Towards a Better Life

Towards a Better Life

BEING A SERIES OF EPISTLES, OR DECLAMATIONS

by

Kenneth Burke

UNIVERSITY OF CALIFORNIA PRESS

Berkeley, Los Angeles, London

University of California Press
Berkeley and Los Angeles, California
University of California Press Ltd.
London, England

© 1966 by The Regents of the University of California
First edition published in 1932 by
Harcourt, Brace and Company, Inc.
Second Edition

First Paperback Edition 1982
ISBN 0-520-04638-2
Library of Congress Catalog Card No. 66-13268
Printed in the United States of America

1 2 3 4 5 6 7 8 9

Preface to Second Edition

The first ten chapters of this novel (or should we rather say, in current cant, "anti-novel"?) were written and published as "work in progress" during the fatal months that were urgently on the way towards the "traumatic" market crash of 1929. The book was completed in the "traumatic" months immediately following that national crisis. And it was published in 1931, when the outlook was exceptionally bleak. Though several competent critics were friendly to its experimenting, the author found that the figures of its sales (or, more accurately nonsales) were also "traumatic."

Originally I had intended to introduce each chapter by an "argument," but at the time I was not able to write those pieces. They were done eventually—and a version of them is included in this edition. Their insertion is advisable because the plot, being told somewhat obliquely, emerges little by little from a background of aphorism, lamentation, invective, and other such rhetorical modes. Particularly in the early chapters, where the narrative strand is being slowly extricated from this somewhat "sermonizing" or "attitudinizing" context, the brief summaries help to point the arrows of the reader's expectations.

The mention of "expectations" brings up another likelihood. I have found that the title of this work can be misleading, if the words are read without ironic discount. I recall, at the time when the book was first published, being invited by Horace Gregory to read portions of it to a poetry club in which he then officiated. The now-deceased poet, John Brooks Wheelwright, who was in the audience, told me of an elderly lady who sat next him. After a while, she had turned to him and asked: "Young man, just *what* is the title of that book?" He answered: "Towards a Better Life, Ma'am." Whereupon she: "Hm! I think it's getting worse and worse." This was a necessary part of the development.

On the other hand, there is also a sense in which an ironic discounting of the title must in turn be discounted. My later study of various literary texts, viewed as modes of "symbolic action," has convinced me that this book is to be classed among the many rituals of rebirth which mark our fiction. And though

I did not think of this possibility at the time, I noticed later how the theme of resurgence is explicitly proclaimed, even at the moments of my plaintive narrator's gravest extremity.

In the last analysis, a work of art is justified only insofar as it can give pleasure. Somehow it must contrive to convert the imitation of ethical liabilities into aesthetic assets. Yet writers often symbolize modes of "purification by excess," designed to "seek Nirvana by burning something out," to call forth a "Phoenix out of the ashes," or to get things entangled in a "withinness of withinness." (I am quoting from one of my later critical books, *The Philosophy of Literary Form*.) To this end they may utilize "some underlying imagery (or groupings of imagery) through which the agonistic trial [that is a bit pleonastic] takes place, such as: ice, fire, rot, labyrinth, maze, hell, abyss, mountains and valleys, exile, migration, lostness, submergence, silence, sometimes with their antidote, sometimes simply going 'to the end of the line.' "

Often, a closer look at such texts will make it apparent that, however roundabout, they are modes of symbolic action classifiable as rituals of resurgence, transcendence, rebirth. Thus, in a moment of extreme discomfiture, the plaintive narrator (our "hero," query), tells himself: "The sword of discovery goes before the couch of laughter. One sneers by the modifying of a snarl; one smiles by the modifying of a sneer. You should have lived twice, and smiled the second time."

So perhaps, by the devious devices of the psyche, these solemnly grotesque and wilfully turbulent pages herald (among other things) the enigmatic inception of an author's devout belief that the best possible of worlds would have the Comic Muse for its tutelary deity.

Earlier, as the reader can learn by consulting the preface to the original edition, I proffered a way of placing this ambitious effort. I'd now want to modify my statement somewhat, as follows:

In its nature as a story that speculatively carries things "to the end of the line," TBL could be classed with any work such as *The Sorrows of Young Werther*. (We are talking of literary *kind*, not of *quality*. And even when it is viewed simply as a kind, we necessarily note: It differs from great Goethe's youthful piece in that it by no means called forth a wave of spellbound suicides.) Also, as is most clearly indicated in the chapter, "Despite them all, in their very faces," the book was written by the sort of verbalizer who had taken particular delight in the "pamphleteering" style of Léon Bloy, (who was pleased to pose for a photograph of himself among his pigs, and who wrote, as early as 1897: "Que Dieu vous garde du feu, du couteau, de la littérature contemporaine et de la rancune des mauvais morts!"). Nor should we forget, as regards the pleasurable accents of gloom, Ricarda Huch's *Erinnerungen von Ludolf Ursleu dem Jüngeren.* (I still keep trying to recall books that had somehow got me.) Then add the fact that the tone of the fourth chapter in particular stems directly from the author's love of St. Augustine's Latin, in the *Confessions.* Later, in *The Rhetoric of Religion*, I returned to that text by a quite different route—and so it goes.

In any event, the book itself is here born anew, as attested by the brute fact of its being republished, after having languished in an O.P. state for thirty-five long (long!) years. Whereupon the retrospective quality of the author's experience has suggested to him some verses that, though they were composed with different thoughts in mind, can be adapted to this benign occasion:

Heavy, Heavy—What Hangs Over?

at eighty
reading lines
he wrote at twenty

the storm now past

a gust in the big tree
splatters raindrops
on the roof

By paring a decade or so from the top figure, and adding it to the bottom one, you bring the span of years close enough to the present situation.[1] And whether these early stylistic exercises are storm or bluster, they are of a sort that, for better or worse, their author could not now contrive to unfold again.

And so it goes . . .

K. B.

Andover, New Jersey
August, 1965

[1] The verses will appear in the March, 1966, issue of *Poetry*.

Preface to First Edition

The first six of these chapters were published in *The Dial;* the seventh, eighth, and ninth in *The Hound and Horn;* and the tenth in *Pagany*. They appeared under the title of Declamations; but though they now have another title, the present version is substantially unchanged. The remaining eight chapters are here printed for the first time.

Originally I had intended to handle this story in the customary manner of the objective, realistic novel. To this end I made a working outline of plot, settings, incidental characters, and the like, before attempting to write any of the chapters in detail. But when I sat down to follow my outline, a most disheartening state of affairs was revealed. Three times the expectant author began, with two men talking in a room, an illicit "dive" in Greenwich Village. These men conversed for a fitting period, telling each other a few things which it was very necessary for the reader to know; a bell rang, the waiter's steps could be heard going down the hall, a peephole was opened; next the slinging of a bolt, then the unlatching of the iron grate; the newcomer, after low-voiced words at the door, could be heard striding along the hall; he entered the room where the two men were talking; "Hello," he said—and for the third time your author tossed Chapter One into the discard. Thereupon he decided that he had best read the signs. And if, with Chapter One barely started, the thought of the projected venture became appalling, the signs very definitely indicated that some fundamental error in procedure was involved. For I had by now written enough to know that, were this to turn out the most amazing book in the world, it could not, as so written, serve as a vehicle for the kind of literary experience which interested me most and which I was most anxious to get into my pages.

Lamentation, rejoicing, beseechment, admonition, sayings, and invective—these seemed to me central matters, while a plot in which they might occur seemed peripheral, little more than a pretext, justifiable not as "a good story," but only insofar as it could bring these six characteristics to the fore. These mark, these six mark, in a heightened manner, the significant features of each day in our secular, yet somewhat biblical, lives—and what I most wanted to do was to lament, rejoice, beseech, admonish, aphorize, and inveigh. Yet I found that the technique of the realistic, objective novel enabled one at best to bring in such things "by the ears." Or rather, I found that whereas these characteristics can readily be implicit in the realistic, objective novel, one cannot make them explicit, one cannot throw the focus of attention upon them, without continually doing violence to his framework. Thus a different framework seemed imperative. So I reversed the process, emphasizing the essayistic rather than the narrative, the emotional predicaments of my hero rather than the details by which he arrived at them—the ceremonious, formalized, "declamatory." In form the resultant chapters are somewhat like a sonnet sequence, a progression by stages, by a series of halts; or they might be compared to an old-style opera in which the stress is laid upon the arias whereas the transition from one aria to the next is secondary. However, much emphasis is placed upon the transitions within this static matter itself, as one follows the ebb and flow of a particular sonnet though this sonnet "interrupts" the story in the very act of forwarding it—or, as in the case of the aria, the aria delays the drama, but once the delay is accepted, we may pursue the development of the aria's theme into other aspects of itself.

I have described my changing of the framework as a decision reached by logical steps, but the process was really much more confused. In the books I had especially admired, I had found many desirable qualities which threatened them as novels—and in liking these qualities unduly I had already betrayed my unfitness to write a novel. I could readily remind myself, by considering the world's arcanum of prose, that the conventions of fiction as developed in the nineteenth century have enjoyed prestige for a very limited stretch of time; and I would not have to look far in search of precedents which gave both a guidance and a sanction for radically different concepts of what constitutes desirable prose. And if I could always, when a writer had contrived some ingenious mechanism of suspense, if I could always, when he had thrown equal suspicion upon nine different people, the heroine among them, if I could always at this point find it quite natural to lay down the cunning volume and never think of it again, what good would it do me to attempt writing in a form wherein this aspect of appeal naturally flourished? I would not dare speak ill of discipline, but to discipline oneself in a field wherein one was so hopelessly outdistanced not only by lack of ability but even by lack of interest, would have been an absurdity. Clearly, I was entitled to read the signs, confining myself to the club-offer of my Six Biblical Characteristics, the Six Pivotals as I conceived them, and rearranging my work accordingly, always recalling, for my encouragement, the more declamatory manner in which prose was written before (and even after) our first great journalist, Defoe, showed that if one thinks of people enough dying horribly enough in a plague one can get effects enough out of simply saying so.[1]

But there is a further step to be considered. I must impress it upon the reader that many of the statements made in my story with an air of great finality should, as Sir Thomas Browne said even of his pious writings, be taken somewhat "tropically." They are a kind of fictive moralizing wherein, even though the dogmas are prior to the events, these dogmas are not always to be read as absolutely as they are stated.

[1] It should be noted, however, that Defoe points in a direction, rather than taking the direction in which he has pointed —and the work of those who learned from him is quite different from his own, which largely retains the formal characteristics of his times.

What is right for a day is wrong for an hour, what is wrong for an hour is right for a moment—so not knowing how *often* or how *long* one should believe in the dubious aphorisms of my hero, I should say that there is more sincerity in their manner than in their content. *Facit indignatio versus*, which I should at some risk translate: "An author may devote his entire energies to rage purely through a preference for long sentences." And if, like a modern painter painting a straight-legged table crooked to make it fit better into his scheme, I had to distort my plot, expanding it or contracting it, accelerating or retarding, giving undue consideration to some minor detail only to elide a major one, and all for the purpose of stressing my Six Pivotals—I had further to select as the most likely vehicle for these outpourings a hero so unpleasant that the reader could not possibly have anything in common with him. He laments, rejoices, beseeches, admonishes, aphorizes, and inveighs, to be sure, but always in a repellent manner—and thus, though he could lay claim to pursuing, in a heightened form, a set of experiences common to many, his way of experiencing them may be too exclusively characteristic of himself alone, particularly as he lacks that saving touch of humour which the reader wisely and deftly summons to sweeten his own personal dilemmas.[1] He is a very frank, a very earnest, a very conscientious man, in whom one should place slight confidence. He has an enquiring mind, which he converts into a liability, or at best employs industriously to arrive at zero. I can say nothing in his favour except that he is busy, and busy in ways that will add not a single car to our thoroughfares. It is perhaps this predicament he has in mind when referring vaguely to his "insight." I have further chosen, for the purposes of the fiction, to give him a kind of John the Baptist quality, allowing him in his extremity to think of himself as a "fore-runner," though I should be hard put to explain what sort of salvation he fore-runs. He is an outsider, an ingrate, a smell-feast, and who could possibly see the burgeoning of a saviour in such qualities?

By changing the proportions of a very average man, we can obtain a monster. We make him a monster if we minimize, let us say, how he feels when patting his little daughter on her curls or when hurrying to some address with a round of presents, and stress how he feels when fleecing his partner or

[1] The reader may summon it here also, as he chooses. For if my hero lacks humour, he does not lack grotesqueness— and the grotesque is but the humorous without its proper adjunct of laughter.

when, like a male mosquito, he cannot eat, so that his only hunger is for the female. That is, a monstrous or inhuman character does not possess qualities not possessed by other men—he simply possesses them to a greater or less extent than other men. Fiction is precisely this altering of proportions. The fictions of science alter them by such classifications as Nordic, capitalistic, agrarian, hyperthyroid, extravert. The fictions of literature alter them by bringing out some trait or constellation of traits, some emotional pattern, and inventing a background to fit. So science and fiction alike make monsters, though adults have agreed not to call an anatomical chart morbid, confining their attacks to the monsters of art. These monsters are constructed partly in the interests of clarity (as is shown in classical drama, where the depiction of violence, disease, excess, coexists with the ideal of clarity, strongly unbalanced characters more readily displaying the mainsprings of conduct). But there is a second factor which leads us, whether scientists or artists, to evolve monsters. A reptile must consume another reptile to become a dragon, says a Latin saying (*serpens nisi serpentem comederit non fit draco*)—and who would not make himself a dragon?

If one could pay homage to a living master without implicating the master to whom one pays homage, I should pay homage to Thomas Mann, whose work has always and in many ways astonished and gratified me. Whereas Milton was concerned with passion as tempered by reason, perhaps we could say that a basic dichotomy of Mann's work is hypochondria as tempered by reason, hypochondria serving as the impulse to discovery, and reason as the means of revising hypochondria's first excessive statement of the discovery. In this, it seems to me, the author of Der Tod in Venedig and Der Zauberberg offers a very profound modernization, or secularization, of Milton's theology-encumbered pair. It is a naïve habit of some critics, when noting that an author's hero ends in bewilderment, to complain that this author has only bewilderment to offer— but the works of Thomas Mann stand as a sturdy refutation of their claims. His works end ever in a hero's bewilderment (may the critic's deathbed be uniquely otherwise), yet the stages by which the author brings his hero to this point offer something very different from bewilderment. He charts a process, and in the charting of this process there is "understanding."

Each sentence of this short work may strike the reader as an error—and I can make no answer. But should he question the "aesthetic" behind it, I dare protest. Whatever the failures may be, they cannot be attributed to the underlying "aesthetic," but only to my ways of exemplifying it. In considering the past of English prose, and in realizing by comparison with the present how much of the "eventfulness" of a prose sentence is omitted from our prevalent newspaper and narrative styles, we are furnished with authority enough for a "return" to more formalized modes of writing. There is no reason why prose should continue to be judged good prose purely because it trails along somewhat like the line left by the passage of a caterpillar. Why should an author spend a year or more on a single book, and end by talking as he would talk on the spur of the moment? Or why should he feel impelled to accept as the "norm" of his elucubrations that style so admirably fitted for giving the details of a murder swiftly over the telephone and rushing them somehow into copy in time for the next edition of the news? The two billion such words that are printed daily in the United States (to say nothing of the thousands of billions that are uttered) would seem to provide the public with enough of them—and if only through modesty, an author might seek to appeal by providing something else. As for what this "something else" might be, the arid stretches of monosyllabic words and monosyllabic perceptions which, partially engaging a sluggish corner of the mind, pass today as the major concern of fiction, would seem to justify anything unlike them, even to the extent of that *Zopfstil*, that "periwig style," that incredible jargon of non-speech, which the German scribes once so zealously cultivated in their legal documents. Quintilian warns us against orators who, in quest of inspiration, rock back and forth with great assertiveness though they have nothing to assert. By striking such postures as would befit a weighty message, he says, they hope to conjure up a message weighty enough to befit their postures (*corporis motuum non enuntiandis sed quaerendis verbis accommodant*). The risk of absurdity here is obvious. But is not the contrary practice of today as ripe for distrust—that easy wording, that running style beloved of evaders, a method without risk, since it is imperceptible, like a building ordered by a merchant, who wants it devoid of character, knowing that any trait, if too pronounced, might earn it enemies and thus alienate his customers, so the modern precept is to write as one would write a laundry list, shunning any construction likely to force the mind into a choice where there need be no choice. On the virtues of my method

I can insist, since the method is not mine; and I should like to be more emphatic in defence of it, but I cannot without embarrassment grow very militant in behalf of a neglected cause which I have only too fragmentarily embraced (having taken too few steps towards the re-erection of the "structural" sentence, the "Johnsonese" if you will, as opposed to the "conversational" style which enjoys current favour). I must be content simply to offer the present volume as practical evidence of my faith in the forthcoming "turn," away from the impromptu towards the studied, while we leave the impromptu to our barroom discussions and our accidental bumping of shins, where it most delightfully belongs.

KENNETH BURKE

Andover, New Jersey,
September 9, 1931.

Contents

xxiv

Part One

Nunc serpens, nunc taurus erat, nunc cygnus et arbos.

St. Paulinus: POEMA ADVERSUS PAGANOS

I. "My converse became a monologue"

General statement of the narrator's antinomian philosophy. And his corresponding discomforts. Reference to a trip with a friend to whom these "epistles" are addressed. Concern with death (as the narrator meets a man "while travelling south alone"). Foreshadowing: thoughts on destitution. Attack upon friend to whom he is writing, and in whom he sees the lucky antithesis of himself. Close: statement of antinomian ars poetica.

I HAD become convinced that, by the exercise of the intelligence, life could be made much simpler and art correspondingly complex; that any intensity in living could be subdued beneath the melancholy of letters. And I tried to realize that we should all be saviours of mankind if we could, and would even slay one another for the privilege. I felt that the man who strove for dignity, nobility, and honour should have his task made as difficult and as hazardous as possible, and that in particular he should be forgiven no lapses in style. The day was long since past when I drew moustaches on the pictures of pretty women, though I still warmed to find that a new generation had arisen to continue the tradition, to carry on the torch which we had handed down to them. When finding that people held the same views as I, I persuaded myself that I held them differently. And as for bravery: dead upon the fields of glory are millions who would have feared to wear a hat in inappropriate season, so I judged that brave warriors were dirt cheap as compared with untimid civilians. We create new ills, I thought, and call it progress when we find the remedies. Yet I was not without wonder, the non-believer finding a legend of miracles itself a miracle.

On looking back upon one's own life, one may sometimes feel that every moment of it was devoted to discomfiture, marked by either pain or uncertainty, and he may worry lest this day be the very one on which he snaps under the burden and, if not talented at suicide, becomes insane. Yet it is possible that by a constant living with torment, we may grow immune to it, and disintegration will fall only upon those whom adversity can overwhelm as a surprise, making little headway against those others who would accept even prosperity with bitterness. For when I have heard much talk of the world's growing worse, I have known that this was indulged in by persons who had thought that it could grow better. And in any case, the belief in human virtue is no cause to neglect the beating of our children.

I finally came to hold that one cannot distinguish between friends and acquaintances—and from then on, my converse became a monologue. I sought those who would listen, when I could not go without them, and did not scruple to avoid them if ever I became self-sufficient, believing that in these unnecessary moments they would be most likely to do me harm. It is obvious that I came by preference to talk most intimately with strangers, and to correspond with my friends on postcards. I discovered that in confessing a reprehensible act, I would sometimes add a still more reprehensible interpretation—and whereas I might forget my own judgments upon myself, those in whom I had confided would carefully store them against me.

Not as by accident, but rather as though some voice had called me, I would awake in the night, and thereafter there was no sleeping. Could vigilance, under these circumstances, be an advance retribution for some yet uncommitted act? Though not by earthquake, people are driven into the street, pawing at one another, gentle and even courteous when necessary, but in the absolute crude, direct, revolting—and it is this panic, or should I say this glacier movement, that must be considered. Did not we two go on a premature search of an already premature spring—and did we not find the skunk cabbages well thrust up, and brooks temporarily crossing the road from every field, while the same Eumenides still rode upon the shoulders of us both? Who, seeing us munch chocolate, would have thought us dangerous? As a precaution, we carried not pistols, but rum. Feeling our flasks against our moving legs, we were assured, aiming to protect ourselves less against the malignant bite of snakes than from the benign mordency of the season. Oh, tender psychopaths—if you be young and one of us, and it is spring, you suffer beneath the triple proestrum of climacteric ("if you be young"), personality ("and one of us"), and calendar (that is, "spring"). I the while being condemned as an apologist; as though he who speaks were more goaded than he who must remain silent! We know there has been a major ill in every stage of the world's history, since we know that in no age were all men sovereigns—but one must sing, though it be but to praise God for his boils. And if I have invited death, calling upon death to take me, I likewise avoided traffic with agility.

Recently, while travelling south alone (and I cite you the episode as evidence of my newly discovered patience), I met a man who attracted me by the obvious disquietude of his movements. As he sat facing me, we were finally able to talk with each other, though the conversation was an unsatisfactory one; for between long pauses, while both of us looked out the window, he would sigh and say, "Death is a strange thing," or "I should not fear to die," remarks which seemed to demand an answer as strongly as they precluded it. The real meaning of this, I came to understand in time, was that he was hurrying to a woman who was near death. After he had spoken at length, and in particular had talked with much penetration concerning suicide, at my suggestion we went to the back of the train, where he explained to me that he was religious, and believed firmly in the process of the Eucharist. Then, as we stood swaying with the car, and watching the tracks untwist beneath us, he said that he had prayed, and that he was sure this much of his prayer would be granted—that he would arrive at the woman's bedside either while the life was yet in her, or before the animal heat had left the body. This, he insisted, would be solace. In circumstances like these, I answered, we may feel the divisions between us: for I could be certain from the way he spoke, that he had thought a great deal upon the matter, and that his preference was a strong one— yet for my part, without the assistance of the death to sharpen my imagination, I did not see how he could feel so niggardly a concession to be the answer to a prayer.

I talked with him further, asking him questions as though he had come from some strange region. And upon my enquiring as to what he feared most of the future, he answered: "Destitution. Destitution of finances, destitution of mind, destitution of love. The inability to retort. The need of possessing one's opposite in years, sex, and texture of the skin; and the knowledge that by this need one has been made repugnant. The replacing of independence by solitude." His reply, I said, suggested that he must be well versed in this gloomy lore. I was sure that had I instigated him further, he could have discoursed with authority on many aspects of fear and undemonstrative disaster, though every conclusion would have been drawn solely from the laboratory experiments of his own biography. With him, surely, each adversity would have its parallel in thought, its ideological equivalent, its sentence. And I knew that the world would hear no more of him. And God pity the man or the nation wise in proverbs, I told myself, for there is much misery and much error gone into the collecting of such a store.

Need one, his eyes shifting with humility, need one who is uneasy on finding himself in two mirrors, need one whose pity of mankind is but the projection of his own plight, need such a one relinquish however little his anger with those who cross his interests? Would a gifted daisy, from thinking upon his crowded slum conditions in the fields, find thereby any less necessity for resisting the encroachments of a neighbour? We must learn to what extent our thoughts are consistent with our lives, and to what extent compensatory; to what extent ideals are a guide to behaviour, and to what extent they are behaviour itself. We would not deny the mind; but merely remember that as the corrective of wrong thinking is right thinking, the corrective of all thinking is the body.

You moralistic dog—admitting a hierarchy in which you are subordinate, purely that you may have subordinates; licking the boots of a superior, that you may have yours in turn licked by an underling. Today I talk out to you anonymously, not because I should fear to tell you this to your face, but because my note of scorn would be lacking. And I would have you perceive the scorn even more than understand its logic, being more eager to let you know *that* I resent you than to let you know *why* I resent you. I would speak as a gargoyle would speak which, in times of storm, spouted forth words.

Further, I have many times changed my necktie to go in search of you and explain to you my resentment, meaning to give you at once an analysis of yourself and an awareness of my hatred—but when I found you, lo! we were companions, exchanging confidences, congratulating each other, and parting with an engagement for our next meeting. I have watched you each year come to consort more irresponsibly with God; I have seen you take on ritual dignity, as the impure take on ritual cleanliness by laving the hands or by spilling goat's blood with the relevant mummery. I have seen you grow brutal under a vocabulary of love. If you wanted to thieve, your code would expand to embrace the act of thieving. Feeling no need to drink, you will promptly despise a drunkard. Nor do you hesitate to adopt such attitudes. Yet he who flicks a weed unthinkingly is heinous, while a crime brewed in protracted spite is pardonable—for the doer, had his equipment been directed otherwise, would have been capable of great pity.

It is true that you are absolved of guilt through your disinterest in these matters, where I am guilty through too much husbandry of my despite. That a stranger, asking us each about the other, would receive from you a kindly, regretful account of my errors, and from me an explosion of venom against you, a credo of vindictiveness which would turn him from me in loathing. This third person, this "disinterested party" (and I already contemn him like yourself) would further think it significant against me that, for every item of good fortune which has been bestowed upon you, he may find in me a corresponding item of failure. But since even humility too consistently maintained becomes a boast, how could I expect otherwise than that my accusations against you should redound upon their author? Yes, I have shouted in still places that this aversion is beyond our clashing interests, that it is not rivalry, but *ars poetica*, and as such would necessarily entail rivalry as a subsidiary, but far subsidiary, aspect.

For all such reasons, and primarily because of my difficulty in finding such an account of my position as would serve also to justify me, I have been silent, until I can be silent no longer. I have waited, trusting that from somewhere would come a formula, which I could point to, saying: That figure is you, and I am this other. But despite much persistent praise of patience, I feel forced into a choice. And I have remained apart from you, that I might not be weakened by your good nature.

Yet there are times, in the very midst of such

11

preoccupations, when my retaliation is of a different order. Our unavowed conflicts, and even my recurrent melancholy memories, seem separated from me, as I find myself busily at work upon my utterance. I would, on such occasions, deem it enough to place antinomies upon the page, to add up that which is subtracted by another, to reduce every statement by some counter-claim to zero. Did each assertion endow with life, and each denial cause destruction, at the close the message would be nonexistent; but, by the nature of words, after this mutual cancellation is complete, the document remains.

II. "If life moves with sufficient slowness"

Opening complaints on life and its injustices. Narrator's envy of his friend. He recounts an incident at a farmhouse, where his friend had become intimate with a girl. Peroration of complaints.

W HEN people are both discerning and unhappy, they tend to believe that their unhappiness is derived from their discernment. For how may we dare solicit the kindliness of Providence, we who in fields and on roadways have killed many bugs? In seeking causes to exist, one should not scruple at the choice of allies, and if noble motives seem weak, let him be quick to hunt out ignoble ones. We may be encouraged to continue purely by the thought that our death or default might give too great satisfaction to our enemies—and the strength derived from this attitude may later be turned to wholly praiseworthy purposes. Life is most difficult for those who are gnawed by the morbidity of justice, particularly if their own ambitions and appetites force them into unjust actions. (Yet I knew a man who was secretly committing crimes against the state, but though conscientious he did not greatly suffer at the thought of treason, for being a magistrate he could discharge his debt to society by the harsh penalties he laid upon even the petty offenders brought before him.) We must be content to possess only as much of nobility as resides in the contemplation of it, while yet remembering that such an equipment will not enable us to live on better terms with our neighbours. The world is made more tentative if all sagacious things are said by despicable people, and all stupid things by the lovable—and wisdom, in becoming a kind of self-appointed martyrdom, constitutes the sage's one claim to coxcombry. Could we, by deliberateness, by refusing to do otherwise, come in time to imagine a less defensive kind of living, and even to acquire something of that geniality which is most intelligently advocated in the books of the sick? Or could we call despair a privilege without implying that mankind should show it preference over happiness when the choice could be settled by a toss? No one's discomfitures are above suspicion, for those who possess neither a great man's power nor his torment, record their own maladjustments at length in the belief that they are somehow displaying the rest of greatness. I mean, by what I have been saying, that knowledge is undigested knowledge; that anything can be contemned, and for good reason; that only those exhortations are of worth which a community could not live by, for he is a shabby moralist who does not outrage the law; that nothing is blunter than a wise rule of conduct obeyed in situations which it was not designed to handle; that the builders of a new continent will learn ways of thinking which serve them well, but which become obstructive once the continent is peopled.

I have considered the highly selected breeds of cattle which are most prized when grossly overweighted with beef, or so hypertrophied and distorted in motherhood that the naturally brief sparing flow of the mammae is prolonged and made excessive, as women in certain regions of Africa are deemed beautiful whose thighs and buttocks have become enormous from disease; and I have realized that men beneath the same sky, with the same readings of thermometer and the same averages of rainfall, are bred to vastly differing environments, so that frailty may be but the outward aspect of exceptional vigour and tenacity. The apparently weak are merely schooled to other strength and may be easily enduring hardships which are intense and even still unnamed, while the man who triumphs has done so by acting in accordance with other rules, like one who would win at tennis by shooting his opponent.

Why! when a great philosopher goes mad, pedants of the opposing schools promptly seize upon his misfortune as a proof of their doctrines—and the people will be convinced, for the world is made logical easily when we link an outstanding trait of a man's character with an outstanding trait of his career.

If life moves with sufficient slowness, or is relentless enough in its consistency for us to awaken day after day upon the same issues, we may contrive to keep our terminology abreast of it, at least to the extent of being able to avow, in written, spoken, or meditated speech, any surrenders which were forced upon us in actuality. What we have been compelled to do, a continuance of the same compulsions makes it easy to admit. Accordingly, it costs me little effort to tell you that I have many times cherished details of your life as though they were my own; that not only in the loose talk of bar-rooms, but in the solitude of my thoughts, I have used such transferences, saying "I" where I should have said "he." I have knelt as you would kneel, though aware that you yourself did not put sufficient content into the posture to find it difficult. On one occasion, when I had overstayed myself, and suddenly realized that the two of you were waiting for me to leave, the abruptness of this disclosure made me feel as though

I had committed some overtly unpleasant act; and I remained still longer, as though to bury it in further sociability. And I have since (by imaginings) stood in that room, and seen the door close behind me, heard my footsteps diminish in the hall and, in your person, turned smiling to my companion. Yet though I have thus drearily mimicked you, I can say with authority that your enviable condition arose from absurdities unperceived, from your failure to hamper your own life by certain self-questionings (self-questionings which insufficiency alone can enable one to neglect, though they usually bring more powerlessness than quality). We were in no outward peril, such as earthquake, attack, or flood, which would have justified your instinctive manner.

Oh, were I to leave some heritage of good counsel for the young, my code would advise the striving after such privileges as are not obtained through deliberation or discipline, but could only be bestowed by hazard. "Go thou, young man," I should begin—and those things which I should tell him to go in quest of, would be such as no quest had ever yielded. By watching you, I learned that blessings fall as manna, which feeds the trivial because the great have prayed. And by unescapably living with myself, I learned that when rewards are commensurate with efforts, they find us already too exhausted to enjoy them and too dispirited through the practice of long patience to feel assured that they will not be taken from us. You drew forth the good things of life like a magician pulling rabbits out of a hat. They came to you, that is, regardless of your character.

But I, who should have considered it my mission to make life more difficult for both of us, laboured instead to continue your good fortune. On seeing you so far entrenched in ways which I myself should have chosen, I was led by a kind of moral pedantry to make those aspects of your career over which I had some influence, remain consistent with those aspects which were independent of me. And nothing so much as the thought of my own unreasoning collaboration confirms me in my conception of you as one unjustly sunned upon and favoured.

Among those times when I lay sleepless, I should mention first our night at the farmhouse. I had not wanted to stop here, yet you insisted. Did you spontaneously know that this was the place for your purposes, or could you have turned any other equally to advantage? I was prepared to go with you to the river, when I observed that plans of your own were already under way. I wandered through the barn alone—and later, coming upon the hired man, I asked him questions about the crops and learned the parts of a harness. It was also at this time that I made friends with the collie, whom I called old Fritz and buffeted into growling good humour. You were now well along the shore, and the hired man explained to me that your guide had returned recently from a convent which, I gathered, she had attended less in the interests of religion than of delicacy. As evening came on, I sat waiting for you in our room, smoking in the dark by the open window. It was a long vigil, preponderantly a period of sound. The clock in the hall struck deep and sluggishly—and after each hour had been thus solemnly proclaimed, it was repeated in a hasty tinkle from the parlour. Our room too possessed a heart-beat, sometimes in the ticking of my watch, and sometimes in my own pulse. "I am waiting," I thought, "like a wife," with the exception that your return would comfort me purely as the cessation of your pleasure. With this girl, I had noticed, there was a slight convulsion of the nostrils, a suddenness of breathing, when certain words were spoken. Yet in so short a time I could not perceive anything in common among these words but their effect, and I took them to betray a state of mind which in its deeper aspects was closed to me by unimaginativeness or the need of longer acquaintanceship. It seemed to indicate a conflict between eagerness and retreat, as though she had included much within her scheme of the repugnant and the illicit, yet by a strong gift of sympathy was made constantly prone to weaken her own resistances.

At last you entered, bearing your disturbance like an emperor. I turned away, that no more might be conceded you, that your expressions should go unseen. "We must leave," you whispered, "leave quietly—not by the hall but through the window and down over the porch." Now we were allies, if not in our adventures, at least in our escape! As I sat up in silence you added, "She is hysterical." We left money by the unlit lamp, and in the yard I proved that I too had spent a profitable evening by having made friends with old Fritz who, at my whispered assurances, permitted us to go unmolested. And as we walked in the grass by the road-side, doubtless even the girl did not know that we were leaving.

Thus the two cronies trudged through the night, while you tossed me the crumbs and bare bones of your evening. But eventually you grew critical, and proved to me at length why this girl was inferior to Florence, why she could not make Florence seem any less desirable, your talk becoming in time one enthusiastic paean to Florence; until, as we arrived at the next village, and learned that you could telegraph there, at your suggestion we sent her our joint compliments and expressed the hope that we would soon be with her. Though I concealed my anger, I tried to make it clear that I was doing so.

There are many now who talk of so standing that the waves alone are in front of them, and the very vessel on which they advance is behind the rim of their vision. And I recall the words of a man (I did not like him!) who saw a great poet, now dead, hurrying along the city streets, suffering from physical pain, and through thinking of other things allowing himself to act as though the stresses of his mind and body could be outpaced. Travellers looking to improvement have gone long distances, changing all the outward aspects of their life, yet finding that they awaken to no new internal dawn. Despite motion, philosophy, medicaments, the one unchanging self remains, to feed upon its store of remembered injustices, of stupidity triumphant, of suicidal worth, of resentments which, though they may lead to the hilarious and the absurd, are none the less burdensome to their possessor. There was even the time when I talked with anguish in a public phone booth, and while Florence listened to words as desolate as my talent and my predicament could make them, I was grinning into the mouthpiece that the man beyond the glass, waiting to speak here next, might not suspect my condition. And on another occasion, when she discovered tears in my eyes, they had been unloosed by nothing more serious than an accidental tap against the bridge of my nose as I stood at the window twirling a curtain string. These trumped-up tears I displayed as evidence of my unhappiness, and I can assure you that they were not inaccurate. They lay in the otherwise stony eyes of one who knows that as a heavy bolt of lightning will, in its discharge, clear an entire countryside of electricity, similarly those near us who absorb good fortune must thereby detract it from ourselves.

III. "This day I spent with Florence"

He recalls his trip through the woods with Florence, and their sitting on a rock together. Describes a play in which Florence and his friend were acting. (He notes with resentment how they flattered themselves by living a fiction, in carrying over their parts from the play into real life.) His envy of Florence and of the friend (Anthony) leads to compensatory boasts of his own, as he tells of his mastery over one Genevieve.

COMING upon the rock, we likened it to a gunboat, or to the crust of some enormous prehistoric turtle, and climbed aboard this monster's kindly back to ride statically through the woods of hickory and oak, and among the scattering of lesser boulders. I, in this early springtime, had not yet learned to distrust the seasonal promises which lead us to mistake exaltation for futurity, and which fulfil themselves not in renewals of our life's texture, not in metaphysical disclosures to correspond with the weather's metaphysical whisperings, not in the quickening sap of changed relationships, but solely in the delicacies and amenities of arbutus, liverwort, and violets protruding through the fallen leaves. I have since found good cause to meet this graceful season with sullenness. Yet I am not one to turn with over-promptness against the uplift of receptivity. I can tolerate in advance that man whom I am later to call a fool; I can make allowance in general for those I shall despise in the particular. Like an earnest woman in pregnancy, I have observed beautiful forms and colours, and listened carefully to harmonious sound, in the hope that such experiences might somehow become incorporate in me and pleasantly affect my issue. And if I now refuse to consider the problematical, it is because the certainty of grimness is preferable to the possibility of disappointment—if I stickle for better prices on Tuesday, it is as one who on Monday bared his breast to the elements.

You and I had not yet taken our trip together, on this day I spent with Florence in the woods. I did not yet have reason to suspect that the subsequent months would prove so favourable to you and so disastrous to myself. We knew that you were at the theatre, reciting your lines as Alcaeus with sporadic energy, waving your right hand as you would later wave it before the audience, while consulting from time to time the still unmemorized script which you held in your left. Surely, of all those details which conspired to assist you, this casting in the part of Alcaeus was among the most momentous. It endowed you with such a character as you could profitably project beyond the limits of the drama into your actual situation. And when on the night of the

première, the emotions of the audience brought freshness to your repeated lines, I soon discovered that
it was not you, but Alcaeus, who walked among us
after the curtain had fallen. Even had we not been
predestined as enemies, this incident would have
remained an oddity between us. I did, it is true, defend you; I could still forgive you laughingly, but
with such readiness that I allowed my resentment to
continue.

Long after the theatre was closed, when we had
carried our conventional celebrating to the point of
ribaldry, you retained your vicarious dignity, tossing off your glass with the defiance of the Grecian in
the play. Thus incited, Florence prolonged her part
as Mary, and sat drinking humbly among us as none
less than the Mother of God. The bar-maids and
kitchen scullions and manservants and apprentices,
all those who had provided the background of ob-
scenity to this theme of intense moral effort, were
still moving about in their costumes—and this was
enough, with their drunken jests and singing which
they had no need of borrowing from their rôles, to
repeat in reality the scene as you and she had acted
it upon the stage. Here was religion for the godless,
the inverted piety of distorting the sacred legends,
the profane worship of those last pillars of the Faith

who painted the image of Christ upon their feet that they might blaspheme him in walking.

The momentousness in the retaining of these rôles came not from the characters themselves, but from the fate to which they had been subjected. Implicit in your mimicry, was the determination to duplicate the plot as well. When the aged Joseph, with his difficult code of purity, has learned the full import of Alcaeus' tirades, has learned that a different avowal of ethical convictions foreshadows a divergent scheme of conduct, and that this Hellenic poet has refused to recognize the barriers of an Hebraic household, we understand the marriage of tetragrammaton and Artemis which was transmitted to the West; like Joseph we see that Mary has been refined by something more subtle than abstention, by exposure to vacillation between opposites, by reverence for both Joseph and Alcaeus at once—so that he may still, when the Wise Men appear at the incunabula of this new faith, confirm them in their worship, while himself compelled to do homage to a purely mental aspect of virginity. The playwright who could conceive devotion under this guise, could readily conceive its dramatic counterpart. Accordingly, as Joseph prophesies (a *vaticinium post eventum* in which he foresees broadly the whole of

Europe's courage under the Christian exaltation), the vulgar supernumeraries enter, to begin their dalliance about the edges of the stage, while Joseph, Mary, and Alcaeus stand apart, untouched—and thus the curtain may fall upon a tableau of contrasted austerity and coarseness. What more, I ask, was needed to bring together two who had borrowed their characters from these sources, what more was needed to give them that illusion of splendour which could make their idyll inimitable?

With fallen branches, as dry and brittle as chalk, and some dead leaves gathered from the crevices, I made us a bedding, where we half reclined and talked. The snow still lay about in irregular patches, like the spots of sunshine that filter through the trees in midsummer. Also, a few of last year's leaves were clinging to the oaks—and it was these leaves now which began to rustle, first far off in the valley under a slow breeze which came upon us a full minute in arrears of its own sound, so that we heard this rustling in other areas while the woods about us were still quiet; thus warned, we could observe the crackling foliage pass from its initial interrupted twitchings into a state of vigorous commotion. The crowns of the trees then yielded, each after its fashion; a few scattered pads of rain fell, visible not as drops but in the starting of dead leaves; and the woods were now beset by a miniature fury so thorough, so all-pervasive, that it even caught at the hems of our coats, suggesting to me in the general flurry the thought that I might, with mock-possessiveness, act as though shielding her in some grave onslaught. We peered studiously into the vacant forest as the breeze dropped away, and everything again became silent, leaving no echo but that in our own minds.

I have rehearsed such miniature cycles as of that day, such minor episodes of ebb and flow which, if our life were a scrapbook, could be cut out and pasted upon a page for me and others to turn back upon, just as I have kept with me a picture of that boulder where we sat. Oh Florence, oh Anthony, call me Florentinus, call me Antonine, as Cato the Younger was called Uticensis for having put an end to his existence at Utica.

I have never consented to console myself with the thought that we may be rich in spirit while tangibly impoverished. Wealth—wealth in love, money, the admiration of oneself and others—is indispensable to those who would surround themselves with the flatterings and stimulations of beauty. Let any one, I repeated in self-admonition, who feels that he possesses some elect insight, make efforts to procure its material replica. As it was once said that the soul, by being enclosed in matter, could not sink below matter, so if we convert our understanding into wealth we shall have an outward form beneath which the inward cannot lapse. Were we to live sufficiently in the past or the future, or in the contemplation of remote ideas, the present could rot without our notice, so that our pretensions to order and repose would be disproved by the repugnance which we should arouse in others. In resigning ourselves to deprivations, we make philosophy another word for envy. Accordingly, I felt that I must acquire much more to retain even that which I already had, as one who would strive for millions to avoid starvation.

There was, in these subsequent months, when I watched the structure of your happiness being erected out of the timbers, the steel and marble, of my despair, one man who felt towards you as I, and we found each other with quick understanding, on our first meeting. He was a sickly and unsightly creature, a mouse-faced man who chewed briskly, and whose enmity of you was cheapened by being part of a general aversion. He hated his employer, his clients, and in particular all laughter which possessed the unthinking ebullience of health. His hostility, despite its constancy, was a blunt and un-discerning thing, content with the scantest of documents. Indeed, in time it came to serve me not as a corroboration, but as rebuttal—for when he had accepted my statements against you, he felt entitled to share them with me like truths we had discovered in common, so that they lost their cogency for me and compelled me to seek new justifications for my complaints. How many weeks did I support this un-seemly alliance, prompted by no motive but the fear of relinquishing it? But when, in his zeal as my col-league, he attempted to expand the field of his deni-grations by including Florence as well, I found the release for which I had been waiting, and tore at him like a fiend, so that we parted company for ever.

Yet I would not have you think that I have been wholly devoid of mastery. I do praise that niggardly configuration of the stars whereby I have been en-abled partially to cancel my frustrations by my deal-ings with another. Though I shared with you but the surfaces of Florence, there is a woman, a certain Genevieve, who has gone to secret places with me, providing me some moments of brilliance and ten-derness. I do glorify my fate that others have thought her lovely, and that her loyalty could thus yield me some portion of honour. What comfort to see gladness in her moist, doglike eyes; what harsh solace to feel her creeping against me in petition! Nor was it an unfair contract. In her I nurtured sinister refinements of which, since she was contented and cheerful by nature, she would have been otherwise incapable. What harm have I done in bringing anguish into a life which was so well able to surmount it, and even to profit by it? Even in trickery and neglect, I knew how to value her, never forgetting that a woman of less delicacy would have been harder to deceive, and that one of no reveries could have added nothing to replace those lacunae in her knowledge of me which I purposely left open. That is, had she been blunter, she would have been less eager to endow me with virtues each time I concealed a vice. For though she thought of me as unyielding, I had constantly made concessions to her— never revealing the details of my difficulties, consistently relying upon her to imagine such explanations as would do me credit, and remaining vague that she might lavish her charity upon me unoffended. You, Genevieve, if at times of a summer evening, when the sun is setting beyond the orchard, and the mist and the indeterminate night sounds are arising, if you go out to walk through the greenish, sea-like woods, I know that the corrosion of your melancholy is not intense, and that it is pure of my own untiring rancours. I know that you walk in sweetness, who believe unquestioningly in moral obloquy, and believe that I have impressed such upon you. As one carves his initials in a tree, so you will bear the mark of me perpetually—and for this also I am grateful. Yes, let life be dogged and weighted down by rigid scruples, that affection, in destroying such resistances, may prove itself imperious.

IV. "My vengeance lay in complaint"

*Memory of preadolescent delight. Then: the furies of
adolescence. His later attempt at cynical "calm." Further
account of his resentment at the way Anthony and
Florence have built themselves a gratifying myth. His
confusion when he tries to attack this myth. How his
attack was invalidated in the eyes of others by Anthony's
statement that he (Anthony) had the money to carry out
the plans for the colony. Closing grimnesses.*

IT IS no dismal trick of the memory that there
seem to have been gentler days in childhood,
lived among animals, and when the fear of death
descended only at nightfall. For I recall little mice,
brought home in a box of cotton, and themselves
warm cotton. I know that we had a parrot which
had learned to say good-bye with exceptional affa-
bility, though generally by way of greeting. And
there were rabbits which I had planned to have
ranging about like sheep, but which the terrier could
not tolerate. This terrier was obstinate, his character
was hardened, he would not change his attitudes—
and since he enjoyed the trip with me to the river,
his interests and ways of thinking were much closer
to mine than theirs were, until his antagonism to the
rabbits turned me also against them. When my
mother at last refused to feed them, they were sold,
and the terrier was allowed to scent his way nerv-
ously through the empty cage. There were also two

pigeons, but though my father had felt of them as squabs, they proved in later months to be unmated, and no vast flock rose from these simple beginnings. I have since, in the city, watched pigeons resting high upon a ledge where, from their appearance, I have judged that they were cooing with a drowsy murmur, a soft flute-note. But the heavy roar of the traffic confined them to a visual subsistence.

There were still other animals, and though I owned them at different times, and in different houses, I can readily imagine them as existing simultaneously, all sitting about me in a friendly, ill-assorted circle, kindly and communicative, comfortable in a New Testament manner of living, and attentive to my preferences. In a toy-shop window I have seen tiny Swiss-carved cows clustered beneath a life-sized chanticleer—and in such simple disproportions these fellows seem to have surrounded me.

What hordes suddenly befell me? By what demonological event was I torn, transformed, plunged into stridency, with my mind henceforth an intestine wrangle not even stilled by the aggressions of external foes? I learn from the study of other records that this change was not abrupt; but to the natural memory, not rectified by documents, it seems so. As the building of vocabulary admitted me to new fields of enquiry, even the work of the philosophers became an ill-poised and unclean thing. Art, letters, the subtleties of affection and longing, the sole factors by which some whit of human dignity might have been made accessible, were surely the foremost causes of my decay. I openly identified myself with literature, and thus identified disgrace with literature. I doubtless brought disrepute upon the guild for deformations which were my own, but which, since I laid such bold-faced claim to art, have discredited in simpler minds this calling whose self-appointed representative I was.

To these responsibilities I have since become more sensitive, being careful to acknowledge as personal stigmata those vices which earlier I should have attributed to my medium. I am aware, however, that many of life's questions have found unseemly answers through being of such importance that they were prematurely asked, while art, by the greater clarity it brings to any subject, may seem to magnify the indecencies which it is enlightening. People who have focused their purposes upon other matters than speech, allowing their familiarity with it to grow by hazard, can condone in practice what would alienate them harshly if spoken. Not considering the breach between thought and action, they can brook no great speculative latitude, and will restrict the possible more jealously than the real. Thus, at least part of the blame must be shifted to my auditors.

While others were devoting themselves to some positive discipline, I made the unwitting choice of looking further into my disasters. Under the slightest of reverses, I would welcome bad weather, would go out to scan a broad, lonely sky at sunset, saying, "This I know; this is a return, a homecoming." Or would stand in places which seemed to prepare me for future misadventures, seeking a process whereby the observation of natural objects might serve as solace. Imagining myself stripped of all hope, all glory, all prospects of learning more and of being fawned upon, I tried to find some resource beneath which I could not sink. For each of the senses, I would note a corresponding external substance—the curving hill for the eye, the smell of birch fires for the nostrils—and in thus considering myself denuded, I have in glimpses understood my privileges. But that man is destitute who, to prove himself well favoured, must glorify his possession of those things which all men have unthinkingly. My awe is rather for persons whose delights are too ingrained for their perception, as with the natives of Tibet whose long inhabitance in purer altitudes unfits them to notice the ringing of thin air.

Me flendo vindicabam: my vengeance lay in complaint. Until I came to practise my unlovely science even in times of greatest comfort. It was accordingly by reason of both this attitude and a lamentable situation that I did, on the night of the *première*, begin explaining my limitations, despite the turbulence and good nature all about me. For I observed how you could share your satisfactions with others, while keeping the causes of them for yourself alone.

To whoever would listen, I explained this subtler kind of injustice, pleading that you had brought them nothing, had admitted them to no real partnership. You had come among us with postures which could easily be proved absurd. Your schemes "for human betterment," your exhortations "towards a better life," were matched by an equally obvious ineffectualness. Such generosity was clearly fostered by the irresponsibility of your position. I approached you, pointedly interrupting you as you talked with Florence, and placing these matters before you. "This idealism is facile and meaningless," I challenged you. "You may advocate much, and thus ally yourself with goodness, through being called upon to do nothing. You need face no objective test. Under the guise of giving, you are receiving."

If only a few had paused to hear me, all paid attention to your answer. "I am prepared to face an objective test," you countered. And they listened without envy while you explained how these unforeseen sums had come to you, and how your plans for a colony could now be carried into effect. Looking at Florence, I perceived that in her mind your previous easy heroism had been corroborated. This disclosure of your wealth was like the sudden unfolding of a new virtue. It was received as integral to your character; coming upon you unexpectedly, it had the quality of a profound accomplishment. But how could I plead such matters, when even in my own eyes I was despicable?

I had lived many years with the vacillations of my thoughts—and these events, while they seemed new to others, were for me but the culmination of my weariness. "I accept," I whispered, though the words were inadequate to convey my wretchedness. In their lame pathos, I was not permitted even the partial relief of an adequate expression for my rout.

Henceforth the relationship among the three of us was definitely established. I, whom people spontaneously called by the surname—you, whom even I preferred to address as Anthony. I saw that I had previously done little to awaken more delicate responses in her: out of my self-questionings, I could offer as my one certainty the fact that I would very much like to have her, thus standing as hardly more than a candidate. If I was incapacitated by my shortcomings, I was made still more so by my abilities. My affection for Florence was too great to admit of caution in my dealings with her; I could not dissemble, since I sought her to endorse and supplement my character. You had appeared among us with ambitions which I had found it convenient to ridicule. But your new resources would now, in the minds of all unthinking persons, seem a guaranty that these altruistic plans would go into effect. Your wealth immediately became engrafted upon your temperament, lending sharpness to your wit and moment to your moodiness. What reason indeed would Florence have for prying into these matters, if prompted by neither adversity nor natural bent? Hypocrisy which does not know itself is, in a gracious woman, graciousness—and the plans which you had explained to her during your time of poverty were pretext enough for her to accept you under your present flourishing. By a sweet logic of the emotions which I could look upon with impatience

39

but not with irony, she would picture the many inducements you might now be able to offer her, and from such an inventory could conclude that you stood greatly in need of her, thus adding the weight of an imperative to what was in itself but a personal preference. I imagined with too great credence these private musings, as she sat alone before the glass, peering into her own eyes, and speaking in a gentle voice to her reflection, "When the time comes, Anthony, I will be ready."

How may one transform his failures into profit, not in the sense of those who leave failure behind them, since that change would involve a profound forgetting, but in the sense of those whose structure of existence is made of the materials of their frustration? I have walked boldly through life, head erect and shoulders thrown back in shame. And when I read of the happiness or sorrow of some one in the tombs of Egypt, when I learn that this name was a sovereign or that name a slave, a kind of silent panic comes over me—for I would not protest against disasters which I knew to be inevitable, but I am troubled by the thought that they might have been readily avoided had I known one trivial rule of conduct which would have altered all my experiences. I become afraid that I may have omitted some slight correctness of procedure, and that this omission has made my difficulties incommensurate to the offence, as with a man who is struck down by lightning through having chosen shelter beneath one, rather than the other, of two adjacent trees. Yet though I consider grimly the spectacle of my own misfortunes, I burst into mild tears at the reversals of a fiction, perhaps because weeping is less a weakness than a danger, and may be indulged when danger is absent. But whereas, through fear of death, one may desire to die, and may find all his interests converging upon this single purpose, such notions are loath to permeate the tissues, and the wish never to have been born is unknown to our organs and our senses.

V. "Unintended colleague"

*He tells of another man who, jealous like himself,
killed himself. The incident happened while all were
celebrating the success of the play. He considers
this man's suicide as a portent of vicarious release.
("He died for me.") How, on the hunch that things would
turn out well, the narrator decided to squander what
few funds were still left. But in the end he must
steal from Florence. In his state of gnarledness, he recites
a catalogue of other gnarled people he has known.*

WE COULD easily retain the quality of a man's voice if his words were uttered immediately in front of us, and but a few minutes later we heard him cry from a distance. Though we may, as I have done, forget the very name and features of this person, we can picture him as he swayed above us in a brilliant room, if we were soon thereafter to see his body lying amorphously in shadows. He exists for me as a voice and a form, since each was abruptly altered.

"We spoke of a little dog," he told me, "meaning a certain lawless portion of her thoughts which would run ahead, or lag, or veer to one side or the other, always experimenting, and living for the future." To expand the metaphor, he pictured the dog as nosing at trouser legs or scattering a school of sparrows. "I had intimated that there was such a dog, and she had laughingly admitted it, though we may have had different things in mind, and I did not dare press her for more accurate definition. 'You will be away from me this evening,' I would venture; 'keep the hound leashed'—all the while trying to decide how much vagrancy I was striking out of her by this method, and how much I was suggesting. Yet I grovelled before her as a tribute to her purity, for in thus grovelling I could better imagine her as pure."

"Such terms are inappropriate to things as they are now," I answered him, referring both to the turmoil at the other tables on this night of the *première* and to the general temper of our age, "and being inappropriate, they cannot lead to anything much more instructive than suicide or murder." When he replied, "In this instance, I can assure you, they will not lead to murder," I was minded to object on the grounds of bluntness, but instead I challenged him: "You speak as though you were here, drinking, with a purpose." So early it was agreed between us that our conversation would terminate in his death, which I took no interest in preventing, despite my sympathy with his disclosures.

He showed the dying man's tendency to summarize, defining himself as "an aggregate of downpours, tides, and crusts," meaning thereby that each sentiment or desire was a commensurable quantity

43

of his body—speaking of the "hellish slaughter going on within me, with various favoured and sacrificed populations, and much hasty rebuilding after destruction" . . . "with the sum total of it all as words," and referring to "obscure processes, the meeting point of Neanderthal ancestors and children yet unborn." Then returned abruptly to the more specific matter: "She had declared with vigour that she would rather live in poverty in Europe than in luxury in America; but by accepting me, for the time being she found herself forced to compromise with her preferences, and live in America in poverty. We did spend pastoral months, however, observing the sun set behind an orchard in a rich documentation of causality and myth. Or we walked together, our elastic shadows turning at the toes. And on cold days we sat in our little house, the smoke from our chimney racing across the fields—we sat in our house, a-sailing. Yet by the end of that season, I feared to touch her, lest it be a fishy hand I laid upon her heart, reminding her of another—I who had lifted her bodily out of girlhood." In trying, it appears, for his sake, to seem a bit more faithful than she was, she had disclosed a slight margin of falsity which he had widened even more eagerly in his fears than she in actuality. He believed himself superior to her in talent and understanding, yet found that her exceptional loveliness enabled her to paralyze him by a mere shift of mood. They returned to the city, and "it was at this time, on glancing into the awry mirrors of a shop window, that I mistook some one else for me. When the phone next door was ringing, I thought it was ours." Explosions, falling over cliffs, trampling by elephants, the birth of an idea (shooting from the head in thick red and yellow rays); a man annihilated by a rejoinder, with nothing left but a few lines to indicate the speed of his departure; the lamp-post wrapped about the neck—at this time he particularly enjoyed that hilarious aspect of distress in which our cartoonists specialize.

"Yet I was not without method," he insisted. "I carefully avoided all traits that might make a demand upon her tolerance. I was not unskilled enough to attempt persuasion by weeping." Tears, he said, were like surface ore: it was readily available, but soon exhausted, so "one must learn to work more low-lying veins which, though harder to exploit, are richer." When she returned to him after a nominal visit to a school friend (and he told himself it was fidelity enough if she returned after flight), he "would sometimes talk of events which had occurred during her absence, advising her to look into certain books I had supposedly enjoyed without her, expressing the hope that an interesting symphony might be repeated, and even on one occasion attempting to suggest that our separation happened to coincide with a milestone in my own progress. I could, with a show of good humour, correct her in the use or pronunciation of a word, or protest that the cut of a garment was too modest." Such discretion served as a stay at best, for in spite of his ability to modify his conduct tentatively, her absences became more frequent. He would open her wardrobe, he told me, "and find her hanging on all the clothes-hooks—or would watch her dainty feet, twelve of them, in a row under the bed. But the smile, and the eyes, were elsewhere." He described her in velvet tones that embarrassed me, "with her knees crossed, and the suspended foot lifting slightly to the beat of her pulse."

Later I came to understand why I connived so readily in his destruction. As he dropped from the balcony, it was like the cutting from me of some parasitically feeding thing. One may welcome defection in his friends, not through the malice of rivalry, but because their disastrous use of qualities held in common argues a greater possibility of a good outcome for these same qualities in himself, since we have learned from the study of numbers that the continued failure of a plan increases the likelihood of its success. "*Incipit vita nova*," he confided smilingly as he left the table for this Leucadian leap into the unseen litter of the courtyard. And I felt that the new life he spoke of was to be my own. "He died for me," I whispered with conviction, though he had not yet descended. And for days afterwards I found myself repeating, "He died for me."

Now I can fully understand the secular certainty which came upon me, leading me to act as though I were protected, enabling me to pattern my life in accordance with your recent announcement, and thus to top each of your expenditures by a greater outlay of my own. There were securities left me by an uncle who had shown good judgment in investing—and in the course of years I had slowly added to them by occasional earnings. They seemed to guaranty me against the last reaches of defeat; I had, when my depression was greatest, got encouragement from the thought of their support. So much, I told myself, was assured me by the organization of a great people who would protect my little in protecting their much. Yet it now seemed that by squandering these bonds I could end my essential poverty. I could look forward to some event, still undefined, which would repay me in both emotional and financial fulness. By spending showily and paying my debts promptly, before my funds had vanished I found creditors willing to trust me for almost as much again. It was several months before the falsity of my belief could be concealed no longer, and I wrote upon a sheet of paper, for my own eyes to read, among designs of cubes and crescents and little running men whose heads and bellies were made by circles, with members and neck each a line: "You are broken." If I then stole from Florence, as I repeatedly denied, I now marvel at the wisdom of this act, which placed some distance between us when I was so thoroughly subject to her. I can be grateful that my predicament forced such accuracy upon me, dictating a form of treachery which, as I now see, was the sole possible manner of rescuing my independence.

The process is now clear to me: How, having died by proxy, I felt that a new era was in store for me; how I had full confidence that the new era would be fortunate, for in being new it would be different from the past, and the past had been unfortunate; how this confidence, by landing me twice over in debt, brought me to such a state that I could steal from Florence. In this devious way I managed redemption, dwarfing the miseries of my love by over-topping them with financial chaos; or we could say that I protected myself from one illness by contracting another, as paretics are sometimes cured by the high fevers of malaria. I understand all this in retrospect, for the knowledge of living is not something to be learned in advance of the calls made upon it; it accumulates with age, matures as its utility diminishes, and under favourable circumstances dies at ninety. We must have haggled with persons since deceased, have sought the favours of the formerly ignored, and received with chill politeness those whose good opinions we once courted. Have repeated in subtler form that process of entering from the cold to stand before blazing logs, or going from the pale of this warm, humming fire into the darkness. Have seen parched ground, then heard a sky split and watched the falling torrents soaked up by myriads of organic and inorganic mouths (this not solely as a meteorological happening, but as a condition among mankind). Have kept our enquiry a little free of our behaviour, that we be not too disrupted on permitting ourselves breaches of principle, since the indulgence of a minor weakness may be our surest way of attaining a major end.

In labelling the lives of other people, we may

persuade ourselves that we are attempting to increase our powers by a wider knowledge of motives. But in this very defence of thought we are guilty of inaccurate thinking. One observes his neighbours, not in a search for usable maxims, but because he can best counteract the memory of past unhappinesses by adopting an aloof attitude towards them, he can best adopt an aloof attitude towards them by adopting such an attitude towards himself, he can best adopt this attitude towards himself by adopting it towards others and transferring it to himself, and he can best adopt it towards others by constant observation, since observation is from without. So I have tried to look upon people as little more than the proof of a thesis, like blackboard drawings to illustrate a proposition in Euclid. A man may have a strange preference for green satin; he may take pride in sending his family each year to the seashore; he may vote the Republican ticket because his father did; he may be doing nicely with his mortgage; by name, address, by his way of gripping a cigar, by the particularities of his experience, he may be distinguishable from every other man and is, of course, strongly aware of his distinguishableness—yet his doctor may think of him primarily as an example of a certain complaint of the liver. So I have given much thought to the surprising mainsprings of human conduct, considering among other things how a slight deflection near the centre can become a wide difference at the circumference.

I have recalled, for example, a poet whose work was exceptional; but restless because he could not write better, he remained enigmatic in his habits, coming from vague places, en route for places equally vague, seen where he was not expected and offering no explanation—and by all this doubtless trying in some desolate way to make his verses still rarer by the rarity of his appearance. And I knew a lonely, introspective fellow, awaiting the pollen of another's charity, well versed in the construction of bridges, but kept ineffectual in his own eyes by reason of his humility in the presence of women. Explaining how one of them, who had forgotten some object or other, returned for it to his apartment where he was alone, "What would you say to that?" he asked me—and I answered, with regard for both the facts and his feelings: "Were five or six such incidents to occur, your two lives might become wholly different," knowing that they would not, as they did not, that his knowledge would be confined to bridges of steel and masonry alone, on which more light-hearted Leanders could keep their trysts in safety. There was a woman so assured of others' kindliness that all who knew her conspired in limiting her experiences to this simpler reality. She sat, I believe, in the shade of an arbour, or in equivalent places, learning of the contemporary through the courtesies of her visitors and the filtrations of well-modulated prose. I could mention another, so little adjustable to conditions other than those for which she was pre-eminently fit, that she was prized by her acquaintances when they were ill, since she could care for them so sweetly, though they found it necessary to discourage her from visiting them too frequently when they were in health and preferred the company of those who, at the time of their need, had abandoned them. Despite divergencies, she resembled a modest clerk I talked with in the West. He had leapt to a position of leadership during an earthquake, showing the abilities of a commander when his superiors were in panic—yet otherwise he spent his life as one tolerated by wife and friends, owing to the infrequency of this disaster. And once, in the springtime, amid a plethora of appleblossoms I caught on the breeze a scent that was meant for buzzards, as an old man lay on the nearby porch dying of gangrene.

My unintended colleague of the suicide had also

told me of his eventual flight: how, as he stopped at a general-store in the country, he was pursued impersonally, by mechanism, since a concert which he knew his former wife to be attending in the city, was recorded here on a raucous instrument. He recalled that a kitten lay asleep, its ear tickled by the rim of a spittoon; he described the crack of billiard-balls, in an adjoining room, at moments foreign to the rhythms of the orchestra; he mentioned a bell which, installed at the door to announce the entrance of new patrons, gratuitously marked their exit.

VI. "The twitter of many unrelated bird-notes"

*Tells of how, by giving Anthony and Florence keys
to his apartment (without telling either that he had given a
key to the other), he set the scene for their union. His
jealousy at the success of his own plan. His gloom as an
"outsider" when he followed Anthony and Florence to
the hotel on the island. The "insight" of money versus
the insight of poverty. His "N'importe où, hors du
monde" escape. The dog barking behind the mist,
and related enigmatic portents.*

W E MAY hold that we would have not one day
of our past repeated—and yet may have been
brought to this view by the repetitiveness of memory. Like a dog leaping after bacon, I continue per-
formances because of their failure. Injustice to another, we feel, is capable of payment, but our mistakes against ourselves seem beyond revision. The
tyranny of even minor social absurdities is not
weakened with time, though its intensity may be disguised by the addition of humour—and we suffer
perennially anew a gnarling of the mind at the
thought of circumstances which once involved the
deeper morbidities of our nature.

When giving Florence the keys to the apartment,
I had not planned to give you the others. It was two
hours after I had left her, with an agreement to meet
her at the theatre the following afternoon, that I
thought of forcing upon you the rôle of an intruder.

54

I found some relief on bringing this blunt element into a relationship which had been too tenuous. And I walked the streets in vicarious triumph, imagining the furnace of your skin as you, to her astonishment, dropped upon the bed, heavy and quick-breathed with drunkenness. There was gratification in the thought that I might derive even my defeat from within.

My plottings seemed to have given me some claim upon her—and when I appeared in later weeks at the hotel on the island, I went to her mechanically, offering myself, without hope, almost without desire, but equally without vacillation. Failure, already predictable through my lack of dignity and absence of gradation, was made inevitable by my diffidence. Yet when I wept, confessing that I had acted by resolve, she was sorry for me, and in her compassion even laid a hand upon me—whereupon I attempted to pursue my advantages, dogmatically translating her caress into encouragement. Her sympathy now gave place to repugnance, as I felt repugnance for myself—yet through many rehearsals of this scene in retrospect, I have come to understand my conduct better, and to see that I had not been undiscerning. I acted through no misinterpretation of motive, but that I might for the moment enable myself to imagine the motive as different. That is:

The hand, laid upon me in compassion, still rested there as I touched her aggressively, and thus was given at least a temporal relation to my embrace.

In the dismal days that followed, I hovered about you that I might spy upon you, not by opening letters and listening at the door, as you might think of one who stole from her, not in things secretly overheard and the bribing of the maid, but by the patient reading of omens, by the effrontery of almost imperceptible changes, by the unwitting expansiveness of her manner. I even found that you spoke in a language peculiar to your own companionship—a separate idiom distinguishable not by the introduction of new words, but by the holding of expressions in common, and by the fleeting reference to many events which others could not understand without further explanation.

I watched the sweet hypocrisy of her plans for the colony. As my own funds neared exhaustion, I observed with fuller realization the powers of your wealth. You could provide material support for those delicacies of thinking which the impoverished, if they happen to possess ability as artists, must generally confine to their medium, and which are denied entirely to all others. You could purchase the elimination of the inappropriate; given your beginnings in imaginativeness and culture, you found an idyll economically obtainable, could back your caprices by ponderable objects, could counteract by external loveliness the lapses between your moments of affection, disguising flaws in the texture of your emotions by covering them with the texture of your environment. While this process was still unfolding, any loss of mutual engrossment would be undetectable.

If one would be receptive without unhappiness, he makes himself dependent upon good fortune. The dignity of great prosperity can be denied only by those who forget that a cathedral can arise out of wealth alone. Wealth and talent being complementary, neither will deem itself enough without the other—and if some men are sought though lacking either, it is only while they hold out the promise of both. Any who write beautifully or speculate profoundly in a hovel are to be commended for the excellence of their product, but unpardoned for indifference to their whereabouts—as their justification for neglecting their furniture would justify others in neglecting them. With wealth there goes a separate biology. I knew one man who had applied his wealth to carrying doubt into his very tissues. As birds, though out of danger, fly with the self-protective darts and veerings proper to their kind, so he kept his statements guarded, even among friends. And I knew another whose fortune enabled him to crowd with affirmations and denials a day which might otherwise have been devoid of both, permitting him to build an environment arbitrarily about him, to maintain a background consistent with the consistency of his own character. Equanimity came easier to you, who could now hire others to bear your annoyances, could by a kind of commercial contract buy off the influences unsuited to your temper. Add the kindred wealth of Florence's affection, and your equipment was complete.

With so much given, I watched you unerringly grasp the remainder. The plans for the colony could follow the rise and fall, not of a colony, but of your courtship. With purposiveness too deep for scheming, you employed them to your personal advantage, discussing a community of cultural interests until you and Florence felt that you shared such, outlining the cycle of a humanistic day until your excursions as lovers seemed the perfect instance of such a cycle, and through your proposals of emotional freedom preparing for her surrender. Is it to be wondered that, once these subtler ambitions were gratified, the plans themselves claimed less of your attention, that the colony should have grown, flourished, and decayed purely *in utero?* The colony perished prior to its inception, because your aims had been attained during its planning.

Oh, maddening trickery, when one may find himself so hemmed by strategy that even his benevolences have an element of cunning—while this man could be villainous under the aegis of nobility. When one may find it necessary to force the expression of his emotions purely that others may understand him rightly—while this man can walk through a tangle of inconsistencies without the scotching of his self-respect. When one, through wishing a fortunate woman ill-used purely that he may befriend her, must be troubled by his own lack of generosity— while this man can, unthinking, situate his boredom in the failure of another to entertain him. Bah! let us endure our minor reversals by inviting major calamities; let us dwarf annoyances, or even melancholy, by calling upon life's entire structure to collapse. I fear that our fate is an aspect of our character, and that even one who dies by accident dies by his own hand.

On leaving suddenly, I sought to abandon the field not only of my humiliating love for Florence, but of many subsidiary jealousies. I returned to the city, where I spent the few remaining hundreds at my disposal, attempting again to live as I had seen you living, but without the too vivid comparison of your presence. Though Florence would have nothing of me, I felt that I had done much to sharpen her interests, and that my removal would prove a disappointment to her. In the city I lived, for the few weeks my funds permitted, in a kind of scandalous affluence, awaiting the unnamable and unimaginable event which would come to rescue me. And when I could disguise my hopelessness no longer, I went to the terminal at midnight, procured a ticket to a town which I had not known, and within an hour was leaving for ever. Reaching the little country station at dawn, in a valley still blank with mist, I stood on the cinders with my suitcase, in the chilly morning air, while the train continued on its way through the valley and the vibrations of the engine diminished irregularly to silence. I noticed then the twitter of many unrelated bird-notes, with the rustle of water somewhere behind the mist—and a dog was barking, imposing fresh sharp sounds upon his own blunt echoes.

Part Two

Thou preparest a table before me
in the presence of mine enemies.

Psalms 23, 5.

I. "I am to Genevieve permanently grateful"

*He is grimly "at home," after having established himself
in a rural setting. Reminiscences of Florence.
Compensatory "use" of Genevieve. Peroration: his
ill-natured philosophy of calm.*

RIGHTLY they cherish their nationality, for the sole distinction they possess is as members of a group. And so great is their desire for conformity, that in an environment of geniuses they might even have shown talent. They are all men of honour when their interests are not at stake—and as their indifference spreads to many areas, the vocabulary of justice still flourishes and exerts influence. On doing them a kindness, if one is too modest in accepting thanks, he finds them prompt to join in the belittling of his services. They preface a boast by avowing their dislike of boastfulness, and before saying ill of a neighbour assure you that they will say ill of no one. He would be a monstrosity among them who did not speak of frankness when speaking with caution, or who would not vaunt his full confidence in another on requiring him to warrant his promises before a notary. For one may commit infractions of their code with impunity, but only by granting the soundness of the code itself. Yet on defending a cause unpopular with them, he will be judged capable of thievery or extortion—and were a murder to be committed they would ask where he had been before they searched for a fiend. One should not, after saying good-bye, turn from them in silence, lest they take his departure as a dismissal of them; rather, he should keep turning to face them, and repeating their own remarks, until he is beyond earshot. I went among them as one rebuked, for there are many things which, if still preserved as echoes, would condemn me. To earn their respect, I left my self-doubts unuttered—and only by keeping my work unseen was I accorded the honours due my profession. Our divergencies being total, I felt no need to reveal them; had they been less, I should have been more liable to altercation. No longer required to wrest an existence from the wilderness, their intolerance for their natural enemies is now trained upon one another. At night the dogs bark in behalf of their masters. The dogs of the different farms exchange challenges—and it is the family units of the countryside proclaiming their isolation.

Since the occasion two years ago when I disappeared abruptly, both you and Florence must think of me as lapsing into silence. Yet for me these long months have been restless with the shouting of many voices. As though housing a fugitive in secret, I have spent clandestine hours with my distress, living among people to whom I could mention nothing. Repeatedly I have speculated upon my unclean courtship, and marvelled at the contrasted accuracy of your advances. Testing the evidence that your affection for Florence was abating, I have imagined the growing tentatives of separation; I have pictured your love, like the heart torn from a turtle, beating after death.

When walking through the country in early spring, you have observed a fresh-cut stump, a massive wound, bleeding its sap into the sunlight. The condition of its baffled roots, severed of purpose, could be the symbol of my predicament. Consider their inarticulate sorrow—yet despite vocabulary my own unhappiness tends to become as puzzled. I have given thought to my bodily well-being, attempting to promote by health a kind of physical certainty which, while not removing doubts, would deprive them of their maximum annoyance. During this self-imposed exile, I know that my eyes have been less eager—not through increased hopelessness, for my hopelessness was always thorough, but through absence of an object for them to light upon. I have thus felt the eagerness die out of my own eyes. Yet could I think of Florence so recurrently without some reciprocation on her part? Could such a giving-out remain unanswered? In speaking her name, I did so with no faith in magic, no belief that the syllables could bring me the reality, but solely because my preoccupations made this labelling imperative. The word did not deny the emptiness about me, though I seemed to have cancelled something by the utterance of it.

Perhaps it is to Genevieve I owe my life—at least to her I owe the fact that this evil was made bearable. In no way could she have been different and served to aid me as she did. Deeply emotional, yet lacking a medium of art in which to embody her emotions, she was compelled to seek her poetry in the disposing of her own person. A pronounced gentleness opened her to another's certitude—and as I gave deep thought to the matter, I saw that, while she was still light-hearted, she was equipped already for her eventual abandonment to my wishes. Thus, I was healed by new designing—and for this I am to Genevieve permanently grateful. There have been months when my delight in her loveliness was exceptional—when a posture or expression astonished me. "Cherish these," I have told myself, as I made efforts to fix them upon my memory. But though I still recall that there were scenes of this nature, their details have escaped me. And on occasions, during our companionship, when I have laid hands upon her, in my enjoyment I have wished that we were at liberty, ranging through a variety of cities, and that I might come upon her by hazard, meeting her in odd places, thereby multiplying this experience under many guises. Was I, in inventing the fiction of my marriage, attempting to help her despite myself, by suggesting an added cause to resist me? Or was I contriving to make her acquiescence more heinous in her own eyes, and thus more a tribute to me—for I had made this false confession previous to my demands as a lover, insisting that she keep it secret. As she did, and she believed me unquestioningly until I myself told her I was not married, when admitting that I had asked another woman of the village to marry me. Had she been strengthened by lack of sensitiveness she would have exposed me, or at least rebuked me, but she received both disclosures without protest.

Can one be said to have misused a woman's gentleness who has always thought of it with gratitude, applying it for the very preservation of his life, and even serving by his praise to make her more gentle?

I assured its permanency by setting an appropriate stamp upon her. Though slighting more obvious obligations, I was scrupulous in the shouldering of remoter ones, for I accepted the responsibilities I had incurred in putting our relationship upon so ambiguous a basis—and that its intensity might be maintained, I spent many hours considering it while she slept. Though she offered to relinquish me, I refused to accept this opportunity to settle the matter so easily. At much inconvenience, I still insisted upon clandestine meetings with her, to shield her from the thought that her own virtues had told against her—and only gradually, with the appearance of speechless regret, I yielded to her insistence upon separation.

During the more tentative eras of the Church, there was a sect which held that one is purified by excess, virtue remaining in the sterile ash left from the conflagration. And similarly we may conclude that there is no inducement in refraining, and all issues must be both met and mirrored, though we may regret that our life was not such as to show this contention to its best advantage. And I should hesitate to compromise a moral by drawing it from my defective living, except that I could not decide whether insight is caused by our faults or exists in spite of them. Thus: if naturally inquisitive, we may find in failure an added incentive to brood upon the norms of justice. Or exceptional wavering may end in constancy, as the waverer learns the quicker to stabilize his conduct without regard for his moodiness. And too great good-will can lead a man to express his arguments vilely since, being too sweet-tempered to hate his opponents, he grows lax in his thinking, and gives us in one volume and for one price both a doctrine and its rebuttal. But even without this confusion, I would ask no one to believe me virtuous, holding that all virginity were best enjoyed alone.

I have sat at the window, silhouetted by the lamp-light, thinking how a prowler without motive could slay me undetected. I have sought the spread of painlessness to further free areas of investigation, rejoicing that I did as the rest of mankind though preferring to do so at some remove from my neighbours, submitting to a self-enquiry maintained without assent, dwelling continually upon my own attributes— a repetitiveness which, though not solicited, is the equivalent of great industry—and by many subterfuges of thought and action bargaining to keep insanity logically submerged.

In summer, during the late sunset, I have walked

my acres (for can I not call that mine which I have earned by marriage), have walked these acres, knowing myself vaguely driven, asking for much, too much, expecting nothing. Vigorous young frogs chirp, doubtless enchantingly, in the swampy portions of the meadows. The trees fringing the crest of the hill show no evidence of wind. And distantly, against the seething of my pipe, I catch a bell, shaken by the cropping of one cow, but announcing the herd. The night patiently descends, with a coexistence of sound and silence which is the quality of expectation, and thus of twilight.

Dare we, on such occasions, feel ourselves on the verge of wisdom, and melt with some kind of theoretic charity as we consider our continent passing into darkness and oceans turning cumbrously towards the sun? One's death becomes preferable to the ultimate destruction or desiccation of our planet. And even the perishing of mankind seems less abhorrent than the thought that profound volumes will lie unread and symphonies be without meaning. I would see all gathered into lore, the defunct vestiges of enthusiasm jealously collated, prizing what has been done against the tyranny of death. There is peace in a sequence of changes fittingly ordered: vegetation is at peace in marching with the season;

and there is peace in slowly adding to the structure of our understanding. With each life the rising of a new certitude, the physical blossoming free of hesitancy, the unanswerable dogmatism of growth. Who would not call men to him—though he felt compelled to dismiss them when they came, communion residing solely in the summons.

II. "How different, Anthony, are the nights now"

Continuing the era of "composure" (composure with reservations!). He contrasts with his present anchorage the earlier period of grotesquely intense suffering (as on the night when he gave Florence and Anthony the keys). We gather that he has married, and is propertied. In keeping with his new "composure," he propounds an ars poetica. And he tells of meeting a scholar who represents an aspect of his own weaknesses.

How different, Anthony, are the nights now, when I leave my family and walk alone, from those nights of my love for Florence in the city. How different in particular from that Walpurgis night when, without your foreknowledge, I arranged that the two of you should share the dark together. On dim, deserted streets I hurried through a city of eyes, under the surveillance of disparate objects which, as I passed, each transferred me to the supervision of the next. And there were real eyes among them, eyes of the cats that paused to note me with distrust (some of the cats stringy, others crouching in bunches behind their faces). As though demons had met to decide the next step in my conduct, and as though, after much heated argument, they unanimously acclaimed a policy for me, I suddenly felt my bafflement give way to one clear desire. I would go, I told myself, and batter at my own door until you came to admit me. I would make my way as in a trance to Florence—and regardless of her attire I would kneel before her. But as I hesitated at the door without knocking, I found a packet of refuse I had earlier placed there—and in the barren hallway I lay down beside it. Such is the grotesqueness of suffering, that I lay down beside this refuse. Then I went quietly away, and all beyond the door was left silent and enigmatic.

Now that this trouble's molten fluids lie buried beneath a crust of melancholy, my walks in the night are short interims between study and sleep. I recapitulate the day, to guaranty the soundness of my investments, be they in lands, cattle, or family. I inspect the remaining centrifugalities of my character, questioning my present anchorage, and in the interests of protection attempting to foresee what possible events could again dislodge me.

This dampened moodiness, this confining of the horizon to my own hills, this blankness of the future—could I not, if differently schooled, wholly accept them as placidity? The frog from which portions of the brain have been abstracted, leaps at each prodding, and when caressed, croaks. The frog, I believe, is happy. Similarly we would drop things from us, to reach haven by a lessening. Yet I am aware that the very caution of our life adds incaution to our speculations, equips us to consider protest, disappearance, abandonment. Where there has been much gnarling of the past, we must maintain equilibrium by leaning.

Ah, one will scheme for his composure. Though none but tainted men contemplate madness and suicide, a certain immunity may result from thinking of these destinies. It is useful to have been morbid in youth, since we learn to bargain for balance at a time when hopefulness was strongest. And when later experiences threaten to overwhelm us, it is as though, having gone mad or killed ourselves before, we could profit by the skill of our past error. Few would perish by their own hand if they waited a fortnight—and surely no one will fall victim to a form of insanity which he abhors. Still, one fears destruction less when he has completed his samplings and knows that he has had a little of all that others have had in great quantity.

By what justice, Anthony, do I write these pages as though for your perusal, when in their very composition I am relieved of the desire to address you? We both share the certainty of words—and one who is at work while his neighbours slumber needs no external sanction for his trade, assured that even a philosophy of despair may, in its couching, become

74

an ornament to living. I pursue these difficulties, knowing that what can cross the mind of one man can be the life-long preoccupation of another, and what can be the life-long preoccupation of one man can become the dominant concern of whole eras and peoples. I would have you join me in lauding the pressure of speech. Consider Voltaire, by nature fawning, open to any bribe, currying the favour of any despot, limiting flattery solely by the measure of his auditor's credulousness, bending to any opportunity, renouncing any principle, yet undoing whole months of sycophancy by a sudden flash of wit, for he could stifle a remark which he considered too malicious, unless he also considered it clever. Each time he retorted to avenge an insult, his words were of so pointed a nature that the structure of the state would groan. It was not his venom, but his accuracy, that aroused the resentment of the court—a splutterer might even have been lovable. It was not his bravery, but his phrasing, that made him intransigent.

A gift is an imperative; a power is a command. It is the successful at love who burn for women, and the articulate who are driven by the need of statement. I would proclaim the musculature of diction. I have seen men of practical accomplishments, harsh in their detestation of thought, who would have terrified me as monsters, and cowed me as powers, did they not proudly display some pun, sickly but of their own making, and insist that their companions show delight in it. There is not one of them but would be an adept at repartee, and withal not one of them fit to apply the sound epithet to a single item of God's universe. I will not allow these weaklings of art to enjoy a jot of self-respect beyond their skill as drudges. He who is impatient of reading, who cannot trace coexistent melodies, who perceives no vast authority in a brush-stroke, is no dog, for he lacks the keen scent of dogs. Whatever our humilities, let them vanish in the presence of such opponents, who merit no encouragement until they have grovelled. Yet I have often left my position unavowed, aware that the self-appointed champions of difficult causes usually display few virtues beyond their devotion, and by their raw urgency will enlist further enmity for the things they advocate.

On my score I have dared quarrel with art, regretting the effectiveness of silence, and of that trickery whereby the sentence most trivial in itself is made weightiest by the assistance of plot—as when a little girl says, "See, the red poppy is in bloom," saying this as an observation of no importance, merely out of pleasure with the flower's suddenness, though the reader knows from past disclosures in the text that the blooming of the poppy is to mark her own death. I have also, in considering art's shortcomings, noted how thinkers, in the codifying of their passions, find names which the thoughtless can appropriate to flatter their own preferences; how men of intensity, dismayed at their excess, give formulae for its cancellation, and these formulae are left to the middling, who needed goads rather than assuagement. However we choose to classify mankind, people must fall into at least two opposing groups, and for one of them the world's best doctrines must be subversive. So we must hold that wisdom itself remains a jungle, and that the most astute advice can fall upon the wrong ears.

Yet have not the most menacing foes of art been its adherents? For if they are not worse than other men, their greater expressiveness makes their vices more apparent. They are proud of their deformities, as an unnatural father, thinking of his child's worth in a circus, might be gratified that it was born armless and four-legged. Still, they are to be listened to, since their unwholesome manner of living brings them an advantage in style over those whose environment is less exceptional. Untouched by compromise, the most ineffectual of them will pardon no lack of greatness in his acquaintances, nor forgive its presence. Yet when they condemn a colleague, they do so not wholly through malice but partly in the effort to keep from repeating him. They are at their best when attacking their own vices in other people. If, on setting out to defend a cause, they find that it impairs their diction, they will defend the opposite. Many of them, who produce little, lay all the blame to the inferiority of audiences, having persuaded themselves that if there were a good echo they would shout at it. And often, before this exile, I have heard them, fresh from their failure to write a sonnet, proclaiming the futility of all culture.

It is, rather, the scholars I would solicit, humble voyagers bewildered in that jungle of wisdom which I have mentioned, equally incompetent in life and among the archives. One I have met since coming here, with an absurdly kindly face, as in some comic drawing of a fruit or vegetable which, by the artist's addition of arms and legs and a few crude lines of physiognomy, recommends itself more to our sympathies than to our appetites. "Raised in an atmosphere of piety," he confided, "denied the correctives of vulgar witticism which are needed to keep the mind of a child wholesome while it is being taught a code of the unclean, I early possessed a structure of theological thinking which left me little desire for companions of my own years. Indeed, my life was given an unreal consistency, for my parents were too scrupulous in their upbringing of me to permit themselves those moments of anger or injustice which would have provided me a sounder schooling. One's childhood should be a closer duplicate of the adult world, should be this later world in miniature—and my parents would have done me greater benefit had they been less exemplary. For my misdeeds I was reprimanded, as neither my mother nor my father would allow themselves to relax in my discipline, and for my accomplishments I was rewarded, with the result that I faced the future with no notion of the tentative nature of our living.

"I will not pause now to explain the perilous years during which I struggled to adjust this early equipment to a world tragically different. Not only would the account of them be inessential, but also they seem by a purposive forgetfulness to have been crowded from the memory. Whereas some things are locked too deeply for avowal, others may be sunk even beyond recollection.

"After the dangers of madness had been miraculously weathered—and only weathered, I believe, by such accidents as a change of scene at the proper moment, or the failure to receive a certain letter, or the death of a dear relative under absurd circumstances—I met a quiet woman of twenty, Margaret, of pious parentage like myself, and equally timid. Though I had by now turned to the most godless of philosophies, and looked upon myself as the negation of what I had been, I soon discovered how much faith within me was still pleading for corroboration, as I had come imperceptibly to place upon Margaret the full burden of these earlier responsibilities, exalting her, and even inspiring her, with theological terms of praise.

"We had gone far in this difficult probing—and both her health and my own, I believe, were being impaired by the strain of our restrictions, when this idyll suffered the irruption of a man who had no patience with such rarity, and perhaps did not even suspect its presence. He was much older, but possessed a certain physical obviousness, and had about him such an air of the expectant as to awaken in those he particularly cared to please, strong suggestions of the future. They would not ask themselves, 'What is our relationship today?' but 'What will this relationship be subsequently?' With others I enjoyed his heartiness, his muscular manner, his wilful judgments, made abrupt and youthful by good health and previous successes.

"I am not competent to describe the change which came over me. But a new factor had arisen, or something asleep was awakened. My love for Margaret, as I had known it, was gone, and in its place I experienced a kind of harshness. Painfully engrossed, yet expert with a new slyness, I watched her transformation at the call of this man. Under the guise of conversational levity, I noted their blazing eyes, their alert bodies, their flood of witty interchange. During banter on the surface harmless, I observed her, tranquil under months of our subtle courtship, now made hectic with consent. The man left soon afterwards, so there was no open crisis. But within a week I too had gone—for that undefined groping of our past could not be restored, and I was not enough the schemer to adopt the tactics of my rival. Yet the incident left me strangely envenomed, and it was many years before I could see that I myself had been at fault."

After a considerable silence, the gloom dropped from him. He faced me briskly, and I saw that he was about to speak with encouragement. "I believe the day will come," and he was prophesying, "when all these disturbances are over, when two people are no more set apart from other men by love than they are by speech, or happiness, or music. The day will come when affection is shared as we now share the elements, when universal gentleness takes precedence over the fierce predilection of one person for another. The day will come—" and at this point his voice became inaudible. Then, with a new beginning: "But will the day come? For people are set apart by art or happiness, just as one interrupts for a moment his exaltation in a concert hall to glance with scorn at a restless neighbour. One cannot feel uplifted without feeling that he is lifted above others. And we share the elements not through virtue, but merely due to imperfections in our ways of ownership. Could sunlight be deflected, the countries of the vanquished would lie in darkness. I mean thereby that we cannot have the softness of great insight, the pardon before offence—or that we can have such only in glimpses. The day, and here I would revise my statement, will never come."

He wept, and I saw that he had wept seldom, for his whole body bespoke weeping—and in its surrender was repulsive as the distorted features partially hidden by his arm. Finally, "As a test of happiness," he resumed, "imagine what manner of life one would impose upon himself were he expiating some great wrong or striving to obtain forgetfulness. Picture existence as it would be under such a theoretical burden, and you will picture the daily habits of us all."

I cherish such meetings, when each man puts his wares upon the table for the other to observe and value. Even while hearing little beyond one's own old soliloquies, he profits by the alterations which a fresh auditor demands of him. However, the two of us have since avoided each other, for both realized that in our first discussion he had brought forth everything he considered of moment, had given me the best cullings of a life which was, in its total, dreary and unpointed. I respected him for his ability to exhaust himself thus rapidly, for though a greater power of multiplication would have brought him more comfort, his aridity made him more accurate.

III. "My exile had unmade itself"

*His sudden alleviation. He recites details of his attempts
at settling. How he even wrote a trivial play for a local
school. How his activity with plays led him to make
arrangements for a troupe of barnstormers.
Among them is Florence. Their incidents together. His
elation and boastfulness (he is now no
longer one with the oppressed).*

How—did I not give great thought to moulding
my career by trivial forms? Did I not vote
for quietude, though procured at the price of ill-
humour and underlying envy? I was set for humble-
ness, adjusting both my mind and my economy to
negative living. Here I have been working to write
out the stages of my resignment—and of a sudden
I no longer need be resigned.

Are there events which one must look upon as
grave intervention; are there changes which, though
unforeseen, are too important for one to consider
them as accidents? Already the things I move among
seem foreign to me. "By what checks could you contrive to remain here?" I have asked myself, watching both wife and children unhappily, as though
there were an unquestionable cause for my departure, known and accepted by us all, as though I
were called away to defend them. These tender fellows—I believe there is much in which I can in-

struct them. Am I permitted to make them of this seed, yet deny them my study of its correctives? Am I not, of all men, obliged to school them in their disease? "By what elation," I have also asked myself, "could you be brought to consider abandoning them?"—and entranced by my own thoughts, picturing my farewell even as I sat surrounded, I felt the encouragement of this woman's pitying eyes. My features, I understood, had shown pain; and I was chagrined at her kindliness, all the more poignant because misplaced. Did she assume that a headache, such as attacked me frequently in recent months, was now upon me? Unwittingly she was rebuking with her solicitations. Though fearing that I might speak in sleep or delirium to wound her, and though trying to imagine some way whereby I could be sure of not doing so, I know that I have daily offered her dismaying evidence of my unrest.

See what I had done in my manner of bargaining. How I had come here, wounded, and been restored by Genevieve. How I had married here, become the father of two children, and erected a structure of citizenship within the requirements of my neighbours— healing myself first by clandestine love, which was dismissed, and thence by some prosperity. Until persons came to me for assistance, which I found no cause for refusing them, so that a further share of good repute was engrafted upon me.

Was there not final surrender, coming with my consent to write for local purposes, a play for the students of the village? A nearby town, smaller than our own, formed the soundest butt for my shameless humour, as the audience was already pledged to laughter by the subject. And there were certain small politicians, routed in the last election, whom it was safe to ridicule. I had known a gentle-minded person who was content to do the bidding of others, but would confront a blizzard at midnight to make certain that his livestock was in comfort. I had wished him all wealth and happiness, but even prior to the growth of his deafness he was silent to the verge of ignorance. I could readily give him nobility in this play. Thus gambling with loaded dice I was assured of my dingy winnings. Thence to a partial office in the school—and thereupon, by resignment too deep for irony, my participating in the cultural improvement of my neighbours.

(May these blunt materials, in this concatenation, trace a more significant destiny. For each unimportant step led to a step equally unimportant, until the last unimportant step, with an outcome which dignified all those preceding it. Oh, vague stirrings at the embarrassed crackling of the knuckles at handshake, for her fingers had been relaxed by travel. Oh, glorious termination of a blind pilgrimage!)

If one, in fleeing, takes the piloting of his life into his own hands; if each modicum of his defence is the reward of plotting; if he digs in a secret hole and buries there at midnight the small coins of his imperfect happiness; and if in a new event, unthought of, he finds that the arrows of his life have changed their course, dare he hold that a gentler existence has sought him out? This they shall not take from me. I have considered them one by one, asking: Is he the man by whom I could be constrained through fear of disapproval—and I have seen that to a *consensus omnium*, as thus analyzed, I was almost wholly impervious.

As we stood above the valley looking down upon the trim grain fields, there was great comfort in the displaying of my acreage. "And the herd?" Florence asked me, "the herd also is yours?" "The herd also," I answered, though this was not exact, for some of the cattle had been sold recently and not yet delivered. But the herd looked smaller from our great height, and my reply was for their proper number as they would have seemed had we been closer.

Let us lie, cheat, dissemble, beg connivance of any, forestall their anger by feigned cordiality should they come to accuse us, ask them kind questions to make their indignation more difficult, praise their despicable children to disarm them; let us cajole, simper, brush hypothetical dust-spots from their sleeves; let us admit all manner of compromise to avoid their forcing of an issue. But should they force an issue I will meet it. They will find such refusal to relinquish, such growling over a bone, as will recall portions of their lives long since stifled, making them go from me with a double hatred. "Do you remember, Florence . . ." I have said to her, thereupon sharing some harmless restoration of our past. Oh, Anthony, this day I confessed how I once spied upon her to learn whether in all ways she was loyal to you—and this confession was a source of amusement to us.

We recalled past acquaintances. "Hubert!" I exclaimed at her mention of him; "I had forgotten Hubert!" And were he here I could have embraced him, though he would have poisoned me for my words. For he had given more thought to making himself unforgettable than ever a Roman gave to fame. I pictured him again, racing in terror from a cow—surely a rabid beast, Anthony, for she came towards us with low-hanging udders, and mooing to be milked. The presence of the herd below doubtless suggested this incident to me. We reconstructed Hubert, who could not share a confidence without fearing that it would be abused, but despite his misgivings could not remain silent. We rehearsed his passion for the worst newspapers and the best literature. His militant fastidiousness, as he quarrelled scrupulously with every servant, discharging his valets for failing to remember constantly the things which he could never once remember. His horror of noises. "Hear it, hear it!" he shrieked, as we were all walking on the beach at night. We fell silent, listening with bowed heads so that the wavelets, working among the pebbles, became intimate. And from far off came the faint, almost purring sound of a motor. "Like a trombone at your shoulder," his sister said quickly, for she knew what was expected of us. "Where shall we turn next!" and Hubert was audibly desolate. Florence recalled his helping her through puddled streets, in his politeness growing petulant when, owing to ineptitude on her part, he could not accommodate her quickly enough. "Yet there was another Hubert," I admonished her, "the Hubert who sailed his yacht in the gale, tacking at fiendish angles, panting from elation and physical strain, and howling lines from Beowulf above the storm." There were two Huberts, a land-Hubert and a sea-Hubert. And how different they both were from his crony, whom we also met here, with the sorrowing face of a hound, the victim of his gullet, sighing from the effects of his last meal, showing the reliques of some past sensitivity now reduced to appetite—gentle when not morose from his burden—and peaceably accepting his daily martyrdom of omelettes and pork as he hastened to his grave. Parts of him drooped upon other parts, as though a body's flesh were held firm by cords and all the cords of his body had been severed.

If we must have a slogan, let that slogan be the present. To move vigorously through chill water, and stretch like a snake in the sun—to do this actually, and to do the equivalent as regards the subtler pleasures of the mind—such is gratitude to Makers. If I built a house, I should want the house to stand self-assertively, at peace with its placing. Let us then be as though builded. Let man take each brilliant day as one dropped from an eternity of silence. Let him enjoy the unique organization of his hulk. Let him be rained upon, wind driven, sunned, firm-footed—living first among the elements and shaping his other experiences by this immediacy. Surely no flower protests at withering in the autumn; even subsidence can be a purpose—and days of gentle ecstasy might bring us to welcoming our decline.

Henceforth I will look upon no man with envy, since he is but repeating in his terms what I have discovered in my own. Nature has become the carpet of our sportiveness. Here is a skilful seller, recommending under many guises, repeating in the sound of birds what is suggested by stirrings of the air, maintaining by sunlight what is likewise proposed by the smell of damp soil, cradling the eye by the forms of a hill to make equivalence for the rushing of water. True, there are frogs, young and incautious, which land betimes in the belly of a heron. The heron's song is not their song. There are the sacrificed—there are those for whom the world was not created, but I am not one of them. For long I have hunted—and now I am feeding. Perhaps I am content.

Those who are to drudge beneath the earth, in the mines, the sewers, the stench of tunnels—let them be bred as other than mankind, give thought to the monstrous preparing of their characters as to their sinews. Teach them that alleviation is neither possible nor to be desired, instruct them in hoglike appetites, nurture their brutality as we encourage in others affection. Do them at least this minimum of justice. Study them that their denigration may be thorough. Guide them downwards.

My exile had unmade itself. Learning that a com-

91

pany of actors in bad circumstances was touring the adjacent counties, I brought *The Merchant of Venice* to this village. Upon the troupe's arrival I noted with relief that Portia was beautiful, and a second later I saw that she was Florence.

Often in recent years I had climbed the hill to which I now guided her, crossing the blunt, timbered ridge, and winding by a briary road into the next valley. Here are the ruins of an old house, among deserted meadows, the rim of hills making it a separate world. It is a lonely spot, where in summer the trout stream sinks beneath pebbles. I have gone through the littered rooms, opened musty cupboards, and rummaged among rags with the rung of a broken chair. I have examined this decrepit house, waiting—and into its dismalness I now guided Florence, that her bright curiosity might give it different echoes. Leaning in the doorway, looking down upon the rotted flooring of the porch, we talked with some gravity. "For every man," I told her, "there must be something towards which he would make his way across dead bodies." And cautiously, never without obliqueness, we discussed our feelings towards each other.

IV. "Let this be a song"

Paean to the excitements of love, due to Florence's reappearance. He thinks of various people whom, for one reason or another, he could include among his band.

IN AN age of tumult, we might best command attention by speaking in whispers. In this age of tumult note how I, gratified, raise my voice. Let this be a song, the learning-burdened lyric of one who, without hope, was relieved of illness. Like some character of legend, he fled from one country to another solely to escape danger, and in the second country became a sovereign. If, living in the city and awaking at night, one were to arise, dress himself, and go into another section of the city; if he, as though guided, were to stop at a destined house hitherto unknown to him, were to mount the stairs, and choose a door among many, knocking for admittance and saying to those that opened, "I am here"; if he should never return to his former bed, but lived another life, with other people, and greatly enjoyed this, or if he found customary places made miraculous, he would be doing in his way what I have done in mine.

In this period of respite, I feel as though I were spying upon my own alien felicity. I learn, Anthony, that I was not greatly unhappy when I used to watch you with Florence—and thus the present, in becoming kindly, has placed even my past difficulties in a kindlier light. If there are processes in the body whereby the memory of sorrow is imprinted in blood, nerves, and pigment, if there is an observable parallel in my tissues so that, with the proper instruments, we could test for prior gloom by an histologist's analysis, then I believe we should find these symptoms suddenly reversed—ducts, formerly dry, must now be flowing, to fill me with biologic unction, and others must have dried which were once dangerously profuse.

I do not neglect the fact that this is error. I do not maintain that, were human living fitly managed, this exaltation would be necessary, or even possible. I say only that mankind has added sums for many centuries, that there are grave mistakes lost among the figures, and that accordingly one more mistake is needed if we are to arrive quickly at the proper total. I say that, given conditions as they are, precisely this kind of illumination was required. And I see no good reason why I should not somewhat discourage those who still are as I was—while among my former enemies I believe I could now find cronies. Do not think, Anthony, that what you cast aside I have salvaged. These are shores previously known but to lizards. Only by the records of citizenship is Florence the woman who was once your woman. It is virgin soil that I have opened up, though you might say I have come upon a settlement. You might say I follow in your footsteps. How—is that not grossness? If one seeks new metaphors, will he not also find new women? I am not tricked when she confides that she preferred me always, though it is useful to our happiness that she should believe this slogan and feel her months with you as little more than an apprenticeship. Nor have I openly called it a deception, choosing to keep such accuracy to myself and not to stickle if present facts cause her to misread past ones. I shall permit her to invent whatever fiction she likes for bolstering up this momentous reality. In love, Anthony, I believe we were like elephants.

People may slay themselves through sheer lack of want—not in despair, but in gently letting their rich blood. We should distrust the tenacious of living, for they are unappeased. Death, if luxuriously managed, has but this one thing against it: that unlike love, it does not well up anew. Yet we must watch, under prospering conditions, lest we be without the guidance and good taste of fear. He who commands a large salary thinks little of boring his neighbours. And if we have spent the best of our years in repairing our defences, we may find ourselves unequipped for times of peace. So I am aware that my good fortune may cancel past proclivities and leave me at zero. To this extent I am already grown shrewd, and like a pawnbroker before lending on a pledge, I hold up our affection to the light, hem, shake the head in doubt, and stroke the chin. I would not have chosen to live in a dungeon, but since I have lived in one so long, I may get a prison pallor in living elsewhere. Should such prove to be the case, we are forced to seek misery as better fitted to our talents.

What man of character has not at least two selves, one desiring to be bound and the other without encumbrances? And now that Florence is with me, the recalcitrant fellow must be heard occasionally. Must I not admit that were we living in a whole pigeonry of contentment, there would be times when it rained, and as it grew dark I should slip out to walk back and forth, along a deserted road?

But hold. In the midst of my paean—and I sought to sing paeans cautiously—I have become disloyal to

Florence. I shall return to her, with doubled attentiveness, and in apprehension, lest she has been equally subversive. Thus can one's distrust of another grow from defects in his own reliability. Yet he may be trained to such bargainings, as I am sure that she is not. And were she, during my absence, to have gone as far afield as I in speculations, then I am back with the dismalness of my damned dungeon.

To you I shall not catalogue the excellencies of Florence, since you would but misread the privilege of your priority with her. Whatever aspects of her I discovered, you would think yourself remembering. I shall only say that she is not avid of admiration, for she has not lacked it. Yet despite many hours devoted to frankness, I have retained so much of policy that I contrive to compliment her as a peer, revealing nothing of my awe. Though I have not bluntly questioned her as to her life since leaving you, she has given me to understand its profit. For reasons which she has not yet made clear to me, she is travelling with these trivial actors, whom she loves with amusement and belittlement enough to make them resentful if they knew it, though I who am outside their group need not be affected. A woman less capable might feel obliged to offer some defensive account of her presence among these moth-eaten fellows, to explain away appearances—but her delight in them, her obvious pleasure in observing their irregularities, places upon me the burden of guilt. That is, if a defence is to be offered, she leaves it for me to discover it for myself, thus making me reproach myself for having thought that any defence was needed. I recognize the steadiness of her position, her confidence maintained without effort. A wellbeing which I had not dared hope for, she accepts as her due.

Well, if she is among strange companions, am I not myself in a motley army? We throng the beaches, we make the noise of frogs, we greet our kind vaguely, smile partially in passing. We go about the roads at night, we are seen talking at corner tables, many of us must feel the half-neglected seasons as obscured by the metropolis, considering spring, not as it lies broadly on a remote meadow, but as seen from an office window. Let me list the group at random. There was a man of seventy who had got for himself a girl scarcely nubile. Some wag called him Goethe. And I knew an unripe druggist who, in drunkenness, would boast of his exceptional sweetheart and then of a sudden grow pale despite the flush of his liquor, fearing that he had made her seem too desirable and might tempt his listeners to follow after him, whereas in reality they were but waiting for him to finish that they might burst forth reciting glories of their own. I might further recall a couple, no more accurately described than as Walrus and Doll. They remained playful, inseparable, and enwrapped until the day of their joint death in an accident. These are among my band, as is the young woman who, though living in dissolute company and herself somewhat dissolute, persisted in chastity. Many ribald and recondite explanations were offered for her conduct, but I felt that she rightly saw in virtue her one distinction. Her closest friend was in great contrast. If a man but made some outstanding name for himself, in an exploration, a work of science, or a potato race, she could not rest until she had shared his bed with him. For the bearers of medals she had the attentive eyes of a dog lying on the hearth of his master. But the uncrowned she forgot like doormen. I should include these very dissimilar women in my band—and the wife of an ambitious lawyer, who cared for her husband assiduously, until he was prosperous enough to leave her and support her handsomely in an asylum after her collapse. And the student, joined in an irregular union with a shopgirl. Their relationship

99

being irregular, he could not summon to his aid the old precepts of fidelity, and he could think of no new ones. I should include the young author who wrote an article in caricature of love, and confided to me that he found love generally on the wane following its publication.

Two people of my band I thought generally abhorrent, owing to the amorphousness of their bodies, the bluntness of their movements, and their sluggishness of mind. On first acquaintance I assumed that they had come together as companions in degradation, but later I understood that they had really sought each other and were delighted with what they had found. And high among this group of my fellow-thinkers were two cultured but slightly morbid men intimate since childhood. Both married, they conceived a dismal plan for testing the fidelity of wives. Each, it was agreed, should attempt the cuckolding of the other, afterwards making a frank report of his experience. One, it seems, was successful, but gave assurance of the wife's great rectitude, whereas the second, who failed, announced success with a show of reluctance.

Dare I go further among this uneven lot? No further than to mention briefly a beautiful, and even picturesque woman, a Madame Durant, loved by two men. Through letters, telegrams, sudden visits, and the intervention of relatives, she carried her drama tumultuously across many states. With her arms about Joseph, she would cry out that she loved Josephus and thereupon, misled by a desire for too literal a symmetry, would cross the room to embrace Josephus and protest her love of Joseph. For to be alone with one of them seemed far greater impoverishment than to be with neither, and whichever she lived with, she thought herself conscience-stricken for leaving the other, though in reality suffering most from a drop in the liveliness of her situation. She wept in contentment, insisting that she was degraded—and friends, stopping to rebuke her for her inconstancy, would become her suitors. On one occasion I drank a toast to her elopement, using for the purpose glasses given prematurely as a present for her prospective marriage to the groom now temporarily abandoned though on hand to bid her and his rival farewell—and I left in complex cordiality, loving her, her two men, her dog, and the darkening inhospitable sky which matched my lonesomeness.

In these multifarious ways they prepare themselves for oblivion, utilizing as best they can their few clear years out of vagueness. But all, all are like the receivers of a legacy, who would keep their good fortune to themselves while sharing with others their delight in it. It were better that they were destroyed at the peak of their intensity, as boys stamp out insects in conjunction—or like the man struck down by an unanticipated bullet as he was smiling to himself, so that he passed without gradation from delight to nothingness, and was dead before the signs of pleasure died on his lips.

V. "Despite them all, in their very faces"

How chemicals bring solace. But love is superior to chemicals. "Good things have been brought to me on a platter." Plans for the future. Enjoyment of nature. Amused recollections of the past. He caps his delight by a tirade against any that would belittle it.

FOR four purposes men have had recourse to drugs: for happiness, phantasy, intensity, and sleep. In the chemical subterfuge of morphine some have for a time found happiness, basking in the glow of an internal sunlight, sprawling upon the warm sands of subjective shores. By the drinking, or smoking, or eating of hemp, the hashisheens have contrived to make the world about them distorted and exceptional, with the burdensomeness of infinity in its proportions, and with many strange, deceptive shapes and distances. For intensity, for swiftness of movement, for a heightening of sensation almost to the point of pain, whereby the sounds of a symphony may become startling in their sharpness, the harsh alkaloid of the coca leaf has been successfully injected into the veins. And sleep is best induced by several synthetic discoveries, in particular the derivatives of coal tar, which, until their excessive use has destroyed a man, will serve simply by the miracle of their toxins to quiet the nag of the most inexorable miseries, and even bring relaxation to those stone-minded who would otherwise lie for many hours of each night, staring into the darkness, their respiration an unsuspected sigh. For such purposes men have had recourse to drugs—and on many occasions in my life I have felt chemical assistance in one or another of such human blessings necessary. What, before our extinction, dare we expect as earthly glory, if not the benign cycle of these four experiences: a calm delight (morphine) in the sharpness (cocaine) and unusualness (hemp) of our day, and at the end of it (the coal tar drugs), our gently drifting into nothing? And I will tell you, Anthony, that by simply being with Florence these recent hours, I have enjoyed precisely this miraculous cycle. Like a cornucopia spilling its fruits, she has overwhelmed me with such gifts as are the reward of a ripening. I am surrounded, I am laden, with the plenty, the squanderings, the heaping-up, of a beautiful woman's affection. Not chemically, but by the fortunate outcome of life itself, I am drugged.

Why! Good things have been brought to me on a platter. The splendid weather has made us a carpet for our delight. We have studied the processes of a dawn, once by walking in a cathedral-like forest while the sun slowly turned the rheostat of day, and once by emerging at noon from a deep cavern. With Florence standing beside me, I have taunted an echo, and we have both laughed as we heard my words repeated, solemn and enlarged. We watched swans on still water, with Florence noting how the birds are weight and colour, but their reflections colour only (and in the sheer extravagance of our mood, we held that since the bird and its reflection could not be divorced, the reflection and not the bird is causally prior). Each place we visited did not exist until, gleaming upon it, we saw it in our own light. In particular I must remember these occasions lest, in the future, my present exhilaration has abated and my life has again come to seem rigid and unchanging. Then, recalling how the rocklike became liquid, I may realize that though one's trouble seems the logical result of many years' direction, though it be the exact consequence of one's plans and temperament, it can be wholly altered if only the unexpected enter: and recalling how Florence appeared thus unexpectedly, I shall realize that the unexpected can always enter. By the unplanned the planned will be remedied.

Yet was her appearance really unexpected? It seems (and I have told her this) that I had been drawing her towards me throughout the period of our separation, that I had been holding forth immaterial hands to her, that every day of my life I had been trying to make myself into a kind of magnet which, attracting in all directions, would bring her to me even though I were not facing her point of the compass when I knowingly or unknowingly called her name.

This-poor devil has advanced, Anthony. He is genuinely lifted up. For he need seek no new thing, unless he discover that only by a new thing can he repeat such moments of pleasure as he has already had. But the apprenticeship to his present masterhood was arduous. I shall not forget the years when he would subtly beg of unknown women, and find solace in touching of them lightly. Ah, melancholy ineffectualness, retreat of snail's horns! I will say that in that era of his dismal adolescence, when he was without anchorage, he fed constantly upon such shamefaced, unavowed, and unconsummated promiscuity, and he will always harbour some vague gratitude towards those who, in their slight suffering of a gloomy and uncertain suitor, while remaining at once kindly and aloof, at once touched and intact, did serve by this ambiguousness, this oxymoron of their conduct, to keep some tenderness alive in him and to loosen somewhat the wall he was erecting between himself and mankind. There was a time when he learned Polish of a maidservant, purely that they might have something more than her doubtful treasure in common—yet when their studies had ripened to a deeper intimacy, and he was able to ask of her all that she was long prepared, I think, to accord him without this circuitous approach, he turned instead to the composition of a sonnet, poured forth his zeal and his remorse in praise of virtue, and then fell into such self-torment, such exaltation and secret abandoning, as still fills him with pain and pity when he remembers it. Gone is all this, and all akin to it. Gone for ever are those days when, in the very rumblings of his stomach, he seemed to hear words spoken. And we may number him among those who would, with great zest, leave everything as it now is, calling upon the sea to roll, the winds to howl, and the dead to lie in their graves, oh dead.

We have thought of life in a rambling place, as in the castles of mad Bavarian Ludwig—or some fanciful cluster of buildings above the Mediterranean, with rooms on many different levels, and vistas down long corridors, and angular turnings of direction—a selected existence, making for peculiar kinds of thinking, feeling, and acting; a playworld for adults, pleasant with artificial insanity; a rareness of habits, caused not by grave internal canker, but simply by the inventiveness of our surroundings; distinct modes of experience whereby we might be amused at such things as people generally found depressive, and be astounded where they saw nothing. We observed the valley—and as we did so, "I understand why it appeals to you," she told me, in her breathy, teethy diction; "The droop of a horse's head, as he stands in the field at haytime, corresponds with the droop of the hay bulging from the wagon he is hitched to. The cowpaths curve, not by accident, but by law, adapting themselves with modulation to the contours of the land which they traverse, while the frequency and gentleness of their turnings suggests the leisure behind their development. The stream which runs through the valley progresses by yielding." And I repeated after her, "by yielding," since the words of a sudden seemed like a revelation to me, though I was slightly perplexed to explain how she could have come upon a thought more in keeping with myself who, in contrast with her inborn airiness, am climbing out of straits. She, rather, has always seemed as though she were dropping empty cartons in places to which she would never return—order, arrangement, husbandry being unnecessary to her privileged negligence. But I am in haste these days; I accept things in the bulk—and even if there is an apparent incorrectness in the fact that the sentences suggested themselves to her, I shall not attempt to plumb them further. Yet it is strange that she thought of them, since they go with such a man as I, indicating as they do a person who has long considered matters of comfort and defeat whereas with her, I am sure, pleasures are taken without thinking.

No, there is a certain over-satisfaction about her mood at present. She has bewildered me too often by revealing gratifications like my own. She talks vaguely of her delight in living, and proclaims it unnecessarily. But how could I expect her to do otherwise, when I have been bubbling like a spring? I have placarded slogans of enjoyment on all sides of me, and it would be hard to understand how she could fail to be noticeably affected by reading them. I have set a pace, and the merest responsiveness on her part should cause her to follow at the same clip. There is, it is true, still some enigma about her surroundings. I do not see why she should be continuously amused by her companions, who are outstanding neither as performers on the stage nor as oddities in their private lives. A band of travelling shoe-makers would be more turbulent and more productive of strange scenes. I do not hold it against her that these people are dreary, but I am puzzled to explain that she does not say so. As for her life since leaving you, there has been some embarrassment between us on this subject. I have been able simply to discover that she is amused to recall your parting, that she has married a man of money, that she has an undeniable affection for him, but on more than one occasion has seized opportunities like this acting tour as a pretext to leave him on amicable terms for a season.

We have discussed the subterfuge of the colony. "Admit to me," I insisted, "admit to me that the plans for the colony became a subterfuge. Admit that they were little more than my learning of Polish. Admit that under a terminology for improving all mankind, he conspired to magnify your relationship. Admit that this match was given importance by trickery, since he persuaded both of you that it was an incidental aspect of a plan having nothing less than the betterment of all society as its aim." I pointed out to her how neatly your general programme could serve your personal ends. In your scheme that experts should live together, each pursuing his special discipline yet exchanging his knowledge with those skilled in other disciplines, you implied your own expertness; and at the same time, in holding that "the dignity of a man is not in his personal attainments, but in the dignity of his vocation," you got yourself distinction by a single sentence. In forbidding the ironical, you seemed charitable while ruling out a technique you were not good at; and in insisting that one should listen without shame to all that others might have to teach him, you were purchasing your own relaxation, as you did also when, though enshrining physical living, you proposed to ban the competitive. Your choice of the "humanistic" as opposed to the "ascetic," was a means of endorsing under a deceptive guise the life of the appetites, thus covertly setting forth the ideas by which Florence would find her union with you reasonable. At my recital of such correspondences she protested with laughter—yet I continued, showing how you both had bolstered up your courtship at the start, you by retaining your rôle as Alcaeus, she by retaining her part as Mary. One loves another, I said, when that other, symbolizing beyond the self, not only is, but stands for. And here you were acting in a play, with such rôles as spread an aura about you (Mary, troubled prettily

by conflicting codes of chastity and acquiescence—
Alcaeus the nobleman, unwavering, persistent, a poet
of eager love). And as the force of this fiction dwin-
dled, the plans for the colony came to serve in their
stead. Thus you could, without boastfulness, even
without your knowledge, be greater than yourselves
—you were parts for the whole, particular for the
general; you were glowing, amorous synecdoches.
"You make me seem huge and bungling," she
laughed, but I would not be put off: "Grant me all
this," I insisted, and she conceded the justice of my
version—and I will tell you, Anthony, that to have
such accusations corroborated is very soothing, for
one is not quite at rest when he has accounted for so
much nobility by trivial mechanisms.

However, I did not primarily deal with you. The
disclosing of your impostures was incidental. In the
main, our times together have but slightly involved
the explicit undoing of the past. Rather, I have
found the greatest excitement in unburdening myself of my own grotesque experiences. I have re-
viewed the story of my flight: my reckless weeks in
New York after leaving you, and my eventual con-
version by an evangelist on a street corner. I recalled
his group—their differing heights, their diversity of
postures, their range in weight, age, and attitude

(since some hung upon the speaker's lips, some were impatient, and some stood as though hired). I remembered how dissimilarly they opened their mouths when they sang, and yet how proud I was, in my drunkenness, at the man's professional rejoicing; though I did become hurt when, using me as a decoy, he pled for further converts. I had felt that I was sufficient game for one evening and that, having bagged me, he should pack up his holy weapons and go home, leaving me perhaps to the care of the one pretty member of his irregular circle. How much I have given off. I have felt like a full sack of grain, pouring its contents through a slit. And though I have listened oftener than this account would lead you to suppose, even in listening I have been unburdened.

Bah! I could continue to announce my happiness thus openly, with a free heart, did not the question of adversaries enter. But how speak out simply, when one must at every turn forestall refutation? At peace, at peace!—damn you, I say I am at peace. Should any man who also writes, see these words and choose to belittle them, I pray I have the opportunity to know of it, and to look into his own productions—for I believe that he is vulnerable enough even were one not vindictive, but with the cutting-ness of vengeance added, one could surely carve him as with a knife. If you, Anthony, or any others of your competent brood, see cause to smile at my elation, I pledge myself to examine their accomplishments until I have made clear all insufficiencies in them, pursuing them with pamphlets, pasquinades, scurrilities, obtrectations from the sewers until, even though I fail to bring a corresponding disrepute upon them, and work rather to my own detriment, I shall have made them embarrassed and uneasy, and shall have given them a catalogue of their unfitness which, however they may smirk in public, they will secretly fear to be exact. In particular there are some who would give the appearance of great vigour merely by using the speech of toughs, and would make us gasp at their courage each time they brave a rain of blows on paper. Their Klondike morality is for the flabby with comfort. Justly they dislike the verbal equivalent of their intimacies— but despite them all, in their very faces, I will grow lyrical about Florence. If certain events have happened, I am required only to detail these events with accuracy.

VI. "A weary trudging homeward in cold dawn"

*Admits that he has been giving a false impression. He
had not been intimate with Florence. But he now
truthfully tells of their union in a dingy hotel.
His subsequent disinterest and cruelty. He is named.
She tells him of her unsavory life since the
time of his disappearance. His dismissal of her.*

I F I gave you reason to believe that Florence had
succumbed to me, and if I even took considerable
pains to suggest this event as the cause of my elation, I can now admit that I partially deceived you,
though adding that what I formerly misrepresented
has since become the truth. Frankness is not the least
important ingredient of trickery. Even while scrupulously following the facts in a confession, we lie by
altering their stress, by dismissing grave details as a
trifle and making trifles into a cynosure. In this
instance, however, I had intended foremost to convey the nature of my happiness. And in telling you
of my delight in Florence without implying my full
possession of her, I should have caused you some bewilderment. My delight, that is, was precisely the
delight of possession; but since it flourished while
we were still apart, I could best make it clear to
you by inventing its motives. Such record of those

days as might have gone into an affidavit would have been more misleading than the liberties I took in behalf of a profounder accuracy. I simply could not rely upon your judgment—and as an ancient master of the law-courts has taught us, when a man's judgment is at fault, we bring him to correct conclusions by deception.

Take into account, however, one further difference: that the delight is all gone from me. You will not think me so naïve as to mistake mere relaxation for a permanent satiety. You will not think me so unskilled as to confuse a weary trudging homeward in cold dawn with a lasting change of outlook. For such conditions of a few hours, I can make fitting allowances. My diffidence arises from a sounder cause—and to explain it I will here give the record of an evening.

Perhaps it would have required a woman of unusual assurance, and a man much less adept than I in matters of decay, to survive the setting without disaster. For a room so dismal would necessarily bring somewhat into doubt the hostess who had invited her admirer into it. Though she were to be here but for a few days, it was hers for this period— and since the bed she had lain in, the table at which she had sat, and the walls that had enclosed her, were repellent, how could I escape the feeling that some last touch of elegance had been taken from her? The sickly lamp, unshaded, hurt the eyes when looked at, but when avoided gave forth a dirty yellow twilight. The soap-dish, pitcher, and basin on the wash-stand, with the covered jar on the floor beside it, played too prominent a part in the haphazard furnishings. The splendid leather travelling bags, standing in one corner, reminded me of her smart arrival as she stepped from the train, yet in doing so suggested that she had not kept up to this beginning; while recalling this startling moment of a few days before, they made me think of a parade, all flowers and streamers as it advanced to band music in the sunlight, but much bedraggled after being caught in a shower.

"Your Portia is not well surrounded," she said defensively as she anticipated, rather than detected, my glance about the room—and I felt some poignancy in her being, of a sudden, *my* Portia, as though by this possessive she were trying to drag me down with her. But I was not in a mood to prize unfavourable details; I hastened to collaborate with her, throwing all criticism from my mind and setting myself to be as elated as I could by the events of the next few hours. "When I was young," I said, "a little girl with a name I had not liked proved so delightful that she has to this day made her name seem lovely to me. So perhaps even this kind of sorry place will hereafter be appealing to me since you have passed here." But I saw that she did not enjoy the exaggerated gallantry of my tone. As I had not praised the room in spite of its appearance, she probably preferred that I had praised it—yet had I done so, I believe that she would have been equally hurt by my obvious attempt at charity. Accordingly, where both an admission and a denial would have been wrong, I believe that my answer was the better, through enabling us to bring a more minuet-like quality into the scene.

I placed a flask upon the table, and she sat on the edge of her bed, laughing as she held out one somewhat foggy glass and one thick China cup without a handle. We drank a meaningless toast together, our sentences unfinished. She spoke well of the liquor, praising "local talent" when I assured her that it came from an illicit still in this neighbourhood. Thus again, in a simple remark, she showed signs of pleading; for her use of an expression originating among actors served to remind us of her vocation—a vocation whose adepts, generally throughout our history, had construed the architecture of noble verses while being themselves disgracefully housed.

We talked in low tones, partly that we might not be overheard, and partly because of the dreary light. But as the alcohol gradually kindled some warmth in us, I arose, kissed her, and asked, whispering, "May I blow out this lamp?"—to which she assented; and I will say, Anthony, that the change in our mood was astonishing. The miracle of her again overwhelmed me while I patiently, and with mumblings, undid her garments. We were for these moments blessed, as I sought to fix with my eyes her whiteness shifting hazily in the dark, contourless, infinite room. With bungling she opened my shirt at the throat—and when she laid her hand against me I was happy that, through all my doings and uncertainties, I had contrived always with conviction to maintain some bodily firmness.

Since, as we lay in the darkness, we continued to sip now and then at our liquor, the indeterminateness of the evening continued. At times, falling silent, we listened to the disparate sounds of the hotel, which were generally remote and unplaced, and then again were immediately upon us, as when a maid went down the hall to the tinkling of ice water and returned at an earnest hurried pace suggesting that she already knew of her next task. Well, I am expert enough in the sounds of darkness, Anthony, in the varying kinds of damnation and delight that go with wakefulness while others sleep. Those that lie awake are waiting—and what is waiting but a listening for sounds? Yet on this occasion it was my privilege to find a pleasurable engrossment in a state which had only too often engrossed me bitterly. It tickled me to think that the very woman who had provided the misery for my sleepless hours was now here to fill them with a compensatory comfort.

She spoke occasionally of the past, with me asking her many pointed questions in an attempt to understand the exact tenor of her life since the time I had vanished. But as she continued, I became aware that her statements, made somewhat unguarded by the liquor, were not wholly in accord with one another. To my astonishment, I found that by paying close attention I could entangle her in important aspects of her story, though I was careful to give her no hint of my suspicions. Indeed, coming more and more to believe that the discrepancies arose from an attempt to conceal misfortunes, I continually praised her brilliant and carefree existence. Even when I had become thoroughly convinced that she was not telling me the truth, I went on questioning her like a blunt student whose eagerness to learn made him meek and credulous.

Finally I decided that I should, in a devious way, call her to an accounting. She had spoken of leaving you because of her love for the man she had married—but she later disclosed that she had not met this man until many months after your separation from her. I first let her see that this important discrepancy had been noted, but immediately afterwards I acted as though I, and not she, had been at fault. "I thought you had left Anthony because of your love for this other man," I said as though bewildered; "I am afraid that some important points of your story have escaped me—for now I gather that you did not know this man until several months after you and Anthony had parted." I laughed. "Perhaps our liquor is getting the better of me, Florence. I thought I was a more expert drinker—but the things you say seem now and then to fall out of place, they will not remain where I had put them. You must speak more circumstantially, perhaps, to take my insufficiencies into account." She was chagrined, lying silent for some time; but though she seemed tense, she said nothing that would explain away this dilemma. I resumed my naïve praising of her: "Be kind to me," I whispered. "Do not be angry with me if I become befuddled. Let me share simply the miracle of you. I have always lived in awe of your good fortune, which seemed like the corollary of your character, events following a delightful and flattering order for you. You have simply flowered, simply evolved from within, assured that the surrounding world would shape itself to your best interests."

We had been lying supine, each talking into the black ceiling, but now she turned towards me. "Who am I?" she said slowly, with a bitterness that made me understand and regret the cruelty of what I had been doing. "Who am I to dispense charity to another?" And then: "Neal, Neal, John Neal," she cried to me in a voice which, raised in anguish, made me apprehensive of the other guests; "I can make this pretence no longer. See . . . I am broken." Whereupon, after sobbing, she spoke to me with pitiable frankness.

So you hurried a weeping woman, Anthony! So there came the time when Florence was not so much a person, as a stage in your life, and a stage which you had passed through? And first you became more jealous of her movements than before, and next you grew more lenient towards her, and finally you showed signs of impatience with those traits which were most definitely hers? She tried not to be too thoroughly herself, but despite the guidance of an occasional frown, she could not always be certain in what way she was reaffirming her identity. She could ferret out her own characteristic turns of phrase with some success, but the matter of her gestures and intonations was more elusive. She even changed the scent of her powder, and placed the articles on her dressing-table differently, knowing that factors as slight as these could be tyrannical, but Hubert's sister was to follow—and so *punctum*. When she was certain that you had embraced this woman, "I have come to accuse you, I have come to tell you what I know," she said to you, hoping that some consternation would show on your face—but as you remained untroubled, she trumped up some trivial disclosure which she told you laughingly, to conceal her intentions and her dismay. I learn that you gave her money for her return to New York—and that she threw this money upon the floor. But you took up her purse from the table, groping about the floor for the bills, putting them into it, and snapping it shut. I understand why you yourself stooped to pick up this money, perhaps even exaggerating the business of your search and thus permitting her at least to retain some show of defiance in her defeat.

It seems that on her return to the city, a young blood, a pugilist who earned his living by preliminary bouts, ogled her crudely, with the result that she went to his apartment with him. He was at this time in rigorous training, as he was soon to enter the ring against a man whom he was not only challenging professionally, but against whom he also felt much personal spite. Accordingly he treated Florence like some strange talisman which should neither be touched nor left unguarded. He was intensely proud of her, watching his cronies with open distrust when they came to visit him at the apartment. (Such visitors were frequent, since this man was also engaged in some kind of illicit dealings, and had advanced himself from a position as bodyguard among some counterfeiters or smugglers to the point where he was managing enterprises of his own.) He would go for brisk walks in the early morning with her, and enjoyed having her watch him at the gymnasium while he trained—but if she expressed a wish to remain at home, he would lock her in her room, though hiring an old woman who sat with a key outside the door, to release her in case of some such unforeseen calamity as fire. It became a slogan with him that the night of his battle was to be the night of their nuptials. Yet as he entered the room following his victory, his face still besmeared with grime and blood, and as he tossed aside the robe he had flung about his fighting togs, a member of his gang ran in hastily to tell him that police were in the hallway. "You must not be caught here," he muttered—and then, laughing despite the occasion, he stuffed her into the dumb-waiter, piled old papers about her, and ran the car into the basement, from which she escaped to the street through a maze of dark alleys. She did not dare return to the apartment for some days, but when she did return, she found it empty and deserted, with the doors left open. An agent, on discovering her here, became suspicious, but she deceived him by making arrangements for a lease, and by giving him a few dollars of her scant funds as a deposit. She then left hurriedly, going to live in another section of the city. After some weeks she obtained a small part in a mediocre play, and has since then been bettering her position slowly. But in this revision of her former story, she made no mention of the man she previously spoke of having married.

Florence is a hunted thing, Anthony—so much in need of kindness that to gain a confidant she sacrificed a lover. I believe that towards the end of her story she fully realized her mistake, for she spoke faintly, with a mixture of illness and despair. But some vindictiveness on my part would not permit her this indulgence. I made her repeat each low-spoken sentence and fill out every innuendo, though I had understood her meaning perfectly.

"If we should meet again, Florence," I said to her, "I pray that it may be possible for us to recover the great intimacy of this evening"—thus, under the guise of a wish for our later reunion, suggesting that I took her departure without me as a matter of course. Several times I mentioned her leaving me. "I understand," I told her, "that in our advancing years the accidents of our position outweigh matters of emotion, however grave." And I even ventured to forgive her for placing such considerations uppermost, though I alone had brought this element into the conversation. I spoke cautiously, with much greater concern for her feelings than would appear from this summarized account, where I am emphasizing the purpose of what I said rather than my methods of concealing this purpose. And though I fear that my words caused her great disappointment, I am quite certain that I did not reveal any change of heart: I left her with the impression that I had assumed the transitoriness of this episode from the beginning. Indeed, I even spoke of the great gain in intensity due to its briefness—

though I was aware of the fallacy in my statement and knew that, while any situation can be intense, the richest are those that grow out of long continuance. However, I felt sure that she would hold the more customary opinion in this matter and would thus assume that intensity is something caught on the wing.

Part Three

The wicked flee when no man pursueth
(fugit impius, nemine persequente).

Proverbs 28, 1.

I. "Revealments that come of creation without revision"

He is prepared for the Next Phase, under the sign of a sinking signal. Ecstatic pilgrimage with Genevieve. The spontaneous artist. A devouring of all experience, hectically. Stages: (1) the cult of stone (its self-violence); (2) natural places; (3) cities; (4) New York City—and vision of it sunk; (5) music in New York; (6) Bach's Passion Music in particular. How he induced Genevieve to accompany him. Rhetorical combats with those who had befriended him.

THOUGH lives rarely have the conformity of entire plays, there are possible subdivisions corresponding to the acts of a play. A cycle or constellation of events separates itself from the general clutter—and since it can be classified, we can note its subsidence. The curtain descends upon a partial close, a converging or resolution of some factors. As I said farewell at the station, expressing my hopes of Florence's return in words which formally concealed the permanence of our adieu, I felt that the fundamental concerns of several years had been rounded off and finished. It was because of Florence that I had gone into this section of the country and attempted to reconstruct a new manner of living—so Florence had been primarily the force holding me here. She made me live as though there were a score I had to settle and living were a vengeance. My fear of her had been the beacon for me to steer by.

But now many conditions which I had schooled myself to cope with, were reversed. I had been pushing against a great weight—and with this weight gone, I fell forward. While her train hurried down the valley, I experienced such gloom as terrified me. For even a life of bitterness was desirable as compared with a life without purpose. "You have no reason," I whispered to myself, "for doing any single thing."

Then with clownishness, I marched precisely, turning the words into a military rhythm, making a tune to fit at random, and centering my thoughts upon this arbitrarily invented conduct. For some time I engrossed myself in my mechanical attempt to ward off the growth of melancholy. But melancholy came, like the fog even then rising from the river. Slowly it gathered about me, quietly it sifted through me, and in its deliberateness it seemed as though it had settled here for ever. Pausing at the trestle, I observed in the half-darkness the iron, and stone, and water. As I touched a cold rail I could still detect some vibration in it: but the arm of the nearby signal sank, showing that the track was free. "I will do only what I have to do," I said slowly into the emptiness, but I knew that this place would be henceforth unbearable. For some days I watched myself with distaste, waiting to learn the outcome of my struggle. And I could not have remained even so short a time as I did, except that my propulsion away from here was not matched by any attraction elsewhere.

Might I say, Anthony, that I put myself in other hands? For I dismissed the future. "I will stay if it is possible to stay; but if I leave, I shall leave as one obeying a decree." With this decision I became aware that a process of discovery was going on within me. I knew that I should, before long, feel definitely anchored to this spot or hear some firm call to abandon it. The issue could be decided independently of me: there was a comfort in knowing that I should have only to wait until I was again clamouring for some specific thing. In the interim, I took an interest in chipping crude, unfinished shapes out of stone—dream-figures, obscene at times, or funny, or with various kinds of malformation which made them more detestable than pitiful. Then I would punish the grotesque things by smashing them with one blow of a mallet, though I do not know why I either made them or destroyed them. Thus imperceptibly a new certainty grew upon me. Even as I waited, it was already there, and gaining strength.

There is a serenity of stone, but I would have none of it. In the course of the hasty months that have intervened since the beginning of my new pilgrimage, I have hacked at stone with venom. Let granite be abused, I have said, until its relevant particles drop from it, and it stands forth, a statue. Here is weight for the muscles, hardness to the touch, dimensionality not suggested, but actual. Quick moods are transformed into the resistances and immobilities of gravitational mass. Men, angular, boxlike, weighted—women emergent, arched, melting back into the rock. Men striding vigorously, and motionless—women undulant, and motionless: abrupt actions, cataclysms; all violently changing things, made permanent at the point of crisis. It is astounding to see, hewn out, a movement of the muscles that would not, but for its presentation in our sound documents, ever have recurred.

The works remain uncompleted. We have vanished often, abandoning in hired rooms mute marbles of different shapes and sizes. We have gone away leaving corpseless cemeteries behind us. They are first drafts, in stone. They are the jottings of a note-book, aggregating tons. A little thing, a replica of herself, my companion brought with her from another city, but I hurled it from the window. One does not carry stone—one goes elsewhere, finding further stone to alter. During these recent months, in living and in art, I have sought the revealments that come of creation without revision. Noting how a work could be improved, I have made this improvement the subject of the work that followed.

Despite all I had labored for many years to accumulate by deliberate observation, I am now tapping some store which I had accumulated unawares. What I had watched, bewildered me; but what I had received without watching, fell of itself into a sequence. I had ceased to suffer the impress of the world and was, rather, giving out things from within me. Accordingly, I can better remember the quality of these months than their specific content. I can remember being in astounding places, but they were seen only on the fringes of my vision, as they jutted beyond the edges of my work. I can remember in a general way neat suburbs, melancholy areas where fields have become lawns and birds call among houses. I can remember that we looked down upon faintly peopled valleys, through a calm in which lie distance and death. I can remember stepping slowly into a lake, until my eyes were even with its surface, the water cutting across the eye-balls. I can remember dawns when my portion of the world turned like a sunflower to meet the day. I heard feathery things come forth, variously awakened, while furry things crept into their burrows (though I knew this rather than observed it, working as though mankind hungered for my burden, filling the room with disputes alien to the walls). And finally, I can remember cities, where we walked in the shadows of gulches, were belched upon by deleterious gases, and the very roots of our hearing were assaulted.

In the most strident of these cities, I now am. Mountains, softened with woodlands, weathered into gentleness, slowly yielding their drainage into the valleys, stand without the din of their construction —and so may this city some day stand calm and oblivious of its troublesome amassing. If it must sink to the bottom of the sea before peace descends upon it, may it sink then into deep waters, that subsequent races approach it from above and pry into dimnesses where we are now harassed by glare. Let me, to help them in imagining, here say that in the daytime this city shakes, but at night it hums and is full of secret places.

Why!—from this strident city there have risen sounds so frail, so miraculous and gently assembled, as to soften their hearers into pensive melancholians, for a time leaving them without aggression. I refer to its regiving of great music. Could we not cherish, and even encourage all harsh diseases of our living, if they can make these cautious sounds a medicament? Is it not fortunate that we need soothing, if this is how we are soothed? We are more than banqueted when the slaying of Christ is ritualized in erudite fugues and made elegant by rehearsal. A gorgeous Crucifixion, and surely attended by a greater throng than crowded upon Calvary. "It is finished: my suffering is finished," the basso mutters in his skilled mimicry of the Passion—whereupon strings and contralto linger on this fact, repeating in various ways that yes, the God-man yields, and we may yield. Note how, by eliminating their trivial moments, they have made themselves more ample—how the work, long pondered, comes upon us without the hesitancies and experiments of its inception. Adepts are employed, by threats and hagglings are instructed in duties, are assigned their places with all the clangour and vehemence of a smithy—and lo! out of fear, malice, rivalry, and ill-natured interruptions, is drawn forth the denial of all uncleanness, a broad flowing river of assertion, its parts united in one purpose as it moves steadily towards seas of the mind which lie in a vague remoteness, surging imperatively for this exceptional hour.

When I had known beyond all doubt that I could remain no longer, I went in search of Genevieve and persuaded her to come with me, not by arguments, but by answering each objection in the same words, with the same accent: "You must come." I induced her not by logic, but by corrosion. For some days we were unfamiliar to each other, which made me fear that she might still decide against me. So I talked much of the future, always assuming that she would share it with me, nor was I niggardly in picturing the pleasantnesses which I looked forward to. Finally, on our coming to a room in which there was a little organ, she played me the pieces she had learned when I was with her previously. I asked her to play me new ones, but at the sight of her disappointment I understood that this old music was a way of homecoming, and I hastened to be forgiven. It was on this evening that our strangeness fell definitely away. I surmised that often, while sitting with her husband, she had apparently sought to entertain him by her playing, but had in reality chosen such music as served to reconstruct, in his very presence, the memory of our former times together. Genevieve, how deeply I regretted at this moment the many inappropriatenesses I had forced upon you: that I should have appeared among poor rivals at a time when you were still unformed, and that I could thus by the mere accident of my priority permanently engage your faithfulness. Would that I could give you as much assurance and regularity as your attachment merits, and that I could have profited by you without bringing upon you the weight of this unwholesome paradox: for things being as they are, your fidelity must manifest itself to the eyes of others as nothing but the forsaking of an earnest and admirable man. I have heard of a beautiful woman who went about it daintily to kill her wealthy husband without detection. In this she succeeded, with the result that she was freed of an unhappy ogre and had vast sums to expend as she saw fit. Being a person of refinement, with the sorrow of this crime to prod her, she applied herself to the work of setting up a cultured way of life for many people. With each year she became gentler, more lovely, more skilled in making delightful arrangements for her friends. In the course of a long life she was able to give them such understanding of suavity as would keep them permanently lifted above their previous condition. Thus she had extracted sweetness out of a heinous act—in contrast with our Genevieve, whose virtues have led her into so much that is unpalatable. I will say in my behalf that I have imposed upon myself all possible strictures, that I have done only what I could not leave undone, and that no hungering man need defend his thefts. For we must treat as moral imperatives all acts of injustice that are unavoidable.

In Genevieve I am fortified. Genevieve, I tell myself, will take care of me. It was the thought of Genevieve that enabled me, when crooked people had befriended me, to insult them. She enabled me first to meet them, after my return to the city, and then to leave them with anathemata. Through her I could bring myself to accept the responsibilities of ingratitude—for how could I have been touched by their services without risking inclusion in their flaccid good-fellowship? An attachment among them could persist only because they took indignities for granted. Or were they kept together through their secret detestation of one another, since each, in despising the rest, knew that they were his peers? There are many complexities that would, if taken into account, confound them—but being too blunt to discern these, they attributed their competence to mastery. Their luck they called talent. If they concealed advancement, it was not through modesty, but lest their friends ask too many favours of them. One of them abused himself long after college, thus avoiding alliances until he had reputation enough to marry a person of means. Another, though puny and riddled with disease, would smouch a woman in a dark corner whenever the opportunity presented itself—and he was there upon the right occasion because he was there upon all occasions. Another, though he would turn in disgust from a juggler who dropped one of fifteen objects, would drivel in drunkenness, expecting the forbearance of every one. They helped him because he would not repay their assistance by using, to outmanoeuvre them, the point of vantage into which they had placed him. Not that he was kept loyal by his scruples, however, but by a general ineffectiveness. What he lacked in intelligence, he made up in temperament, and his deficiencies as an artist he covered by a splendid zeal for art. He took pride in his body, which was the caricature of itself. A fourth could be keen only by being frenzied, could be calm only by being lethargic, could show anger only by snarling and pleasure only by wagging his tail. A fifth would sit alone in his room, playing soft music and imagining excesses. A sixth had the convictions of a typewriter. Put it in Moscow, and it prophesies the dictatorship of the proletariat; put it in Washington, and it pleads for low taxes on high incomes.

There was also an expert in righteousness. He admired in his friends the qualities which, should the need arise, would enable one to fleece them, and in himself the qualities which would best equip him to do the fleecing. That is, in them he prized simplicity, gentleness, candour—and in himself a diligent using of advantages or, as he labelled it in his own mind, biologic fitness. He had learned how much one saves, and how reputably one saves it, by over-generous impulses. Through offering a bushel where a peck was lavish, he could end by parting with nothing. As for another: if his companions were walking on the right side of the street and he suggested that they walk on the left, and if they crossed to the left because they did not care which side of the street they walked on, he took their acquiescence as a concession to his authority. For when they treated him with friendliness, he preened himself upon his skill at handling them. He was proud of his clarity when he had little to be vague about—and if he made as much as three where the possible score was ten, he would give his opponent good advice. I did not resent his way with me until I saw it in a dream; for I had never really perceived it until then, when he exposed its workings in all their absurdity by displaying great distinction in the handling of a trivial matter.

They were frank when they found deception too strenuous, smiling when a smile made it awkward for an angry man to strike them, bubbling with attachment to old friends when their attempts to rise into other circles had gone amiss, and never so generous as when praise could be given in lieu of money. Find me a one of them who did not loudly champion justice, while banqueting in behalf of the starving miners—for they knew the value of goodwill, and would not so much as launch a new joke without first farming it out for one night to a Milk Fund. From them I learned that if all the loyalty, devotion, and self-sacrifice were taken out of life, there would still be greed and coxcombry to carry forward the world's best causes. They lacked enough for moderation to come easy—so they answered a loud man quietly, thereby offering a rebuke to him and to themselves a compliment. They would discuss with one another their grave concern for the good of mankind, but would grow black if a colleague, equally exalted, happened to use one of their mankind-saving sentences as his own. The one way to refute them was to cry *tu quoque;* for if you could show that their accusations against you applied to them also, you would be spared in the general amnesty by which they spared themselves.

I arose and exposed them all to one another. To each I delivered his formula, as though on a card registering his weight. To each in turn I shouted, "As for you—" and told him, with specific incidents as proof, wherein he was despicable. Whenever possible I used the words which one of his cronies had said against him—for though they were always carousing together with a show of great conviviality, they were as constantly belittling one another in whispers, with each trying to tickle the others' women unnoticed. They remained friends only because wolves run in packs. "Come, Genevieve," I said finally, and we swept from the room. What cleansing as we rushed into the street, to breathe the sharp night-air—and how indebted I should feel to Genevieve, who strengthens me to live thus without compromise.

Does not this incident show, Anthony, that I had previously wronged myself? I had distrusted my own deprecation of others, suspecting always that it arose from either vindictiveness or envy. But how could I be vengeful, when these people were kind to me, helping Genevieve to support us in the city?

And how could I be envious when I could not, in any important detail, select for myself a different life from the life I am now leading? If I wish for other things, I do so purely as one might wish to be here if he is there, or there if he is here—not as one might very earnestly plead, in sleeping and waking dreams and in unintentional puns, for something constantly denied him. In the past I had not done myself justice. I have been treated hospitably, I am not deprived, yet my despisals continue. Thus, since they spring forth without the provocations of a personal dilemma, since there is no canker of frustration discoverable in them, they are not a comparison, but a vocation. They occur precisely because my terminology best equips me to disclose them. So I must persevere, even at the risk of great inconvenience to myself.

Yet I could as easily have loved these people. As they stood about, half-minded to attack me, each enraged for some specific thing I had said against him though secretly in sympathy with what I had said against the others, I could not have repeated one sentence I had spoken. Even at this moment I realized that for any act, or any way of thinking, there is a tender word and a harsh word, equally applicable. Caution may be called vacillation, acquiescence may be called toadying, sturdiness may be called obstinacy. I knew there was deceit in my using the harsh words only—but unless we adopt a false position, we cannot get our truths stated. What I said was accurate because the zest with which I said it was a lie. In being more honest, I should have conveyed nothing. So, like a ventriloquist's doll, I suffered injurious remarks to rise unbidden to my lips. And I might have confessed as much to them, except that, even as I thought of it, I found myself stamping about the room in a fury and shouting for Genevieve to leave hastily with me.

II. "Mad girl in white"

His jealousy of Genevieve. He experiments to test her fidelity. His jealousy flowers in his symbolic infidelity with a "mad girl in white." His perverse dismissal of Genevieve, and his curse upon himself.

WHEN a casual word reminds a man of an injustice he has done the speaker two years before; or when one mentions a sect slightingly, only to realize immediately afterwards that a member of this sect is present; or when, in talking of a friend behind his back, we suddenly recall that our accusations apply likewise to the person we are addressing—such incidents are marked in an unavowed manner, by a starting up, or by a slight shifting of the eyes, or similarly. Yet, through being exceptionally alert to note when a tiny revealment of this sort has taken place, one may be more frequently misled than the sluggish. For he will feel the need of explaining a transient shade of embarrassment where the relevant information is not available to him, and thus he may fall into a false idea of motives when he could have been better guided through having observed nothing at all. It is accordingly no boast to claim for oneself skill in the uncovering of these subtleties—since one is more likely to find the right direction by striking off at random. For my own part, when I had grown uneasy about Genevieve, and felt that in some tenuous way she was turning from me, I was bewildered by a profusion of data which, though I knew they were symptomatic of something, I could not say symptomatic of what.

It disturbed me that she so often neglected to lock a door behind her, and that she left her little jewel case open. I became worried when she lay awake, for one who had lain awake as often as I, would necessarily fear that she was gnawed at—yet I was also worried when she slept, since in sleeping soundly she seemed to have gone beyond the stage of regretfulness. I was displeased at finding in her too many games and imaginings which were my own, tricks for making familiar places exceptional, jocular references to our separation, delight in the mild confusion of thinking the room turned backwards. "If she decides that my table should be repainted," I told myself, "I shall know that the arrows no longer point towards me." Yet when she did suggest that she be allowed to paint my table, her sweetness was unmistakable, and I secretly granted that if there was any centrifugality here, it could safely be dismissed. Though I knew that in all pertinent matters she would falter, I found it hard, in dealing with such secondary symptoms, to know what faltering was.

Perhaps, I feared, Genevieve does not have morbidness enough for continued loyalty. And since I have got no decorations, what can she point to when, in her thinking, she pictures herself praising me to other women? What was my right to her, when I have made no perfect thing? And how claim her with authority until I have been acclaimed? I found no valid reason why she should be attached to me— and though I might refrain from telling her as much in words, there are surely imperceptible means whereby I must convey this grim truth to her in spite of me. I had been reassured at the thought that she was used to serving me; for in being prompt to anticipate my needs, she became less likely to consider her advantages. She had taken crumbs of kindness from me so habitually that she might not know me for a beggar. "John Neal," I told myself gloomily, "if she but stamped her foot you would, deep within you, scurry away like mice." In returning to her after vicissitudes, I had proved myself subject.

How derive comfort from a woman's power to

delight us when, this power coming from a reservoir of greater possibilities, she is adequate by being more than adequate, and the superfluity may take her from us? Are not women by nature kindly—and so would they not, were nothing else involved, incline to befriend each man that requires them? And does their caution, their withholding, arise not from an abhorrence to surrender but from a desire simply to be as rare as the proprietary lover would have them? Will they, at least, transgress by the slight welcoming of anonymous and slinking suitors? The very forces that bring people together are, by continuing unchanged, also capable of taking them apart. And how if she had come upon a man who, less twisted than I, asked simply that she be wholesome and took it upon himself to supply all else that might be needed in their relationship? Knowing that I could excel in a comparison only by measurements of my own making, what guaranty did I have that Genevieve would not come to base her judgments upon codes more in keeping with other men? And was it not an unseemly state of affairs when the proof of her love for me was in the tears she had shed, and the proof of mine was in the hours I had lain awake, like living stone, endlessly what I am? I had watched, but I could accuse her of nothing. I remained silent through lack of evidence, but also as a rule of thumb: for it was my purpose to hold her, not to win in an argument—and in accusations between lovers, it is a privilege not to be victor, since one gains his point by proving that the other has mistreated him. Once, aghast at a slight disclosure which I have since forgotten, but which seemed overwhelming at the time, I boarded a train to a little outlying town, and spent the day walking swiftly along country roads. "It was a trifle, it was nothing, I could not possibly take offence," I told myself repeatedly, in all manner of ways proclaiming my lack of resentment while I pelted trees with rotten apples and stones.

I considered many aspects of the problem, devoting to it by far the keenest portions of my day. I recognized the blindness of my investigations. I knew that proofs so intangible could be interpreted only by grouping, making details indicative in the aggregate whereas none was indicative in itself—yet such grouping would require a principle of interpretation adopted in advance. And even if I did detect infractions, I warned myself, I should have little to build upon—since she might reasonably be forced into a slight margin of falsehood through trying, for my sake, to seem more demure than she was. "Does he not ask her to be shy enough for the two of them?" I taunted.

I knew a man who, suspecting his mistress of disloyalty yet unable to make certain, finally hit upon this plan: He spent an evening drinking with a somewhat hot-headed friend who was most likely to be informed. To this friend he boasted outrageously of the woman's adoration. "I have put a spell upon her," he said in drunken grandeur, and in various other ways gloried in his unusual prowess until the friend, irritated beyond endurance, leapt from his chair, hurled his glass to the floor, and shouted: "You braggart, I know it for a fact that the woman has deceived you!" I had neither the aptitude nor the opportunity to attempt this subterfuge, but I did in a dismal way experiment. In particular I touched Genevieve suggestively as she slept, calling strange names close to her ear, and cradling her gently. "He is gone now. I saw John Neal leave," I whispered to her. "Now we can be more intimate, because John Neal is gone," while I waited to see whether she would show some dream-sign of welcoming the speaker. I disguised my whispering as much as possible, though one cannot disguise a whisper greatly without absurdity, and I knew that an absurd whisper would be no test since it would not appeal to her in any case. Laying my hand against her, I increased and decreased its pressure in time with the motions of her breathing. At first she made faint efforts at resisting me; but later, to my chagrin, she acquiesced. Yet whereas I succeeded in inducing her to exhale in quick spasms, with her breath a tiny roar against the pillow, I did not know how to make her dreaming reveal itself more distinctly. I understood merely that she was agitated; but when both the sleeper and her tormentor twitched at the harsh sound of a horn in the street, I abandoned my experiments in shame and laid my head gratefully against her shoulder. If I have not been able, Anthony, to show wherein Genevieve is distinct, it is because I have applied myself to questions of motive rather than of character, and the same motive may be common to very different people, since anybody can do anything for any reason. I think that she could satisfy every need in me but the need of some one else.

I have not yet decided whether it is regrettable or fortunate, that precisely at the time of these disorders I came upon a mad girl in white. I saw her at a busy street-corner, apparently engrossed in ravings of a pleasant nature, for she smiled and nodded as though answering very courteous statements. At first I had thought her speaking to some of the people that passed; but on watching more closely to see what sort she singled out, I became aware that her eyes were without focus, looking into a blur or an emptiness that had nothing to do with the irregular traffic in front of her. She was more odd than beautiful, with a litheness that was revealed in the set of her clothing. For some time she walked back and forth on the corner, never ceasing to respond graciously to the imaginary speakers that surrounded her. I happened to have with me flowers I had bought for Genevieve—and taking my cue from her manner, I presented them to the girl with exaggerated gallantry, saying: "These flowers were picked for you. I but perform my duty in bringing them to you." She accepted them without surprise, though she retained her air of preoccupation, neither answering me nor looking at me. In a pleasant undertone, however, she thanked some cavalier of her fancy. I hastened to make other ceremonious remarks to her, suggesting above all the notion that we were conspiring together and shared important secrets. When she finally took my arm, I led her to a dingy hotel near the river, where I was not likely to be questioned, easily concealing the drabness of the place by whatever grandiloquent conceits occurred to me. The burden of our courtly conversation at last becoming too much for her, she fell silent, though walking about our room with great pomp. Henceforth no words were exchanged between us. We moved with pantomimic gestures, in deft retreatings and pursuit. I would at times turn from her, whereupon she came towards me; but as I relented, holding out my arms to her in stylized pleading, she would choreographically renounce me. My eyes becoming tactile, she should have felt them like light fingers upon her shoulders. When we left the hotel, I stepped into a bus with her, dropping back among the crowds on the street as it drove away. She took a seat by the window, and had turned her head towards the aisle in the belief that I was following, when another vehicle closed her from my sight. Thus she had vanished for ever, with her flowing hair, and loose garments, and sinews correspondingly liquid. And I have asked myself: Was this incident the reverse of my uneasiness to do with Genevieve, or did the two have no bearing upon each other?

Oh, Anthony, I am bewildered by these matters, unfit as I am to distinguish between the unstable and the unchanging. I know that poets, to explain any man's excessive conduct, need but attribute to him the entanglements and proddings of jealousy. So much is undeniable, I had told myself: If a woman were long absent, and were sought by a brilliant suitor, and were befuddled by drugs, such convergence of allurements would surely overwhelm her, frailty under these conditions seeming so reasonable that my reliance upon Genevieve was basically shaken. Yet though mastery went from me, and I had been plagued with the fear of losing her, I became calm enough when I lost her in reality. "Hereafter there is no Genevieve," I repeated slowly. Far in the recesses of my mind, as a slumbering possibility, there was great anguish; but no part of me active at this moment felt disturbance. A lucky bewilderment helped me to shut away the thought of her, while I was also aided by my growing intimacy with a man I had met recently in a park. We began talking to each other after he had noted the title of a book I carried with me—and within a few minutes' conversation I had become convinced that he was exactly like me. "You are my alter ego!" I exclaimed. When it came time to leave, we arranged for other meetings here. Yet I would not let him tell me his name, insisting that I should know him as none other than Alter Ego.

Even now I understand, however, that the inconclusiveness of her departure must continue to act upon me. Finding ourselves without funds, I had sent her from our room, telling her that she could get us money from any man. And since I saw or heard no more of her, I can in no way construct her life from that moment. When she left, I regretted what I had said, and hurried to the street in search of her, but she had vanished. Yet I am sure that on leaving she had intended to return, for I cannot recall even a covert means of sealing her departure. And let me say, purely as though deposing, as though the words were being ticked by telegraph, that if I were not myself, but something that looked down upon this that was myself, I should brand it, I should in quietude put an effective curse upon it, I should corrode it with the slow acids of the mind.

III. "Alter Ego"

*Progress of the curse: concerning Alter Ego, who
deserts him. He returns to the country in darkness, but
learns that he has been erased there.
Lonely return to the city.*

ANTHONY, you the nominal recipient of these un-
sent letters, may I who have so often attacked
you, may I now in imaginings turn to you, cling to
you even, relying upon the simulacrum of you I carry
in my mind, wherever you may be, telling myself
that one whom I have addressed so constantly, under
whose eyes in a sense I have lived, is regardless of all
insults my ally, telling myself that affection continues in the absolute, that there can be attachments
underlying deep rancour, and that my very alterca-
tions have given me some undeniable claim upon
you? Oh, I am sorry for every living thing. Could I
not go to you, show you these various items, and say,
laughing: "Why, look at all the harsh things I have
been saying against you all these years, while you
have been going about the world, doubtless happily
enough. Isn't it comic, Anthony—eh, isn't it comic?"
I can imagine myself saying this to you, and imagine
you considering the entire matter without resent-

ment; for inasmuch as you were never from my thoughts, it is not important what I have said against you. One generally has his profitable anchorage, his connections with ways of sustenance, his fireside moments among persons with whom he can feel easy. But those lines that go between a man and others, one by one they were severed—and we may get ourselves to that point where nothing short of genius or luck could uphold us.

I knew a dismal fellow who noted possibilities inexorably narrowing, who with the passage of each year had fewer cronies, less expectations, shorter respite, until he accepted the shelter of a companion much like himself, but moneyed. This man fed him, and said things that, because of the similarity between the two, delighted him. The first was John Neal, and the other we shall call his Alter Ego. But now Neal is quite alone, and I can tell for a certainty how Alter Ego would reassure himself. He would say that I could not suffer so much as I had in advance feared to, that accordingly his disappearance should serve as a relief in that it at least ended my apprehensions. He would say that he had but made the latent patent, the covert overt; he would feel sorry for himself that he, on this occasion, should happen to be the instrument of so natural a process. Into the silence of his room he would speak soft sentences, wishing me prosperity—and he would reproach himself only for not having left me sooner, before I had gone so far in growing dependent upon him. I turned him from me through being in too great need of him. What I should have taken off-handedly, I accepted with deep gratitude. And I had long been sure that my lack of separate strength would tell against me, for I knew that had he similarly leaned upon me I should have found him repellent. I would bring him things which I thought might please him, and sometimes they did please him—but my subservience became obvious to us both.

I cannot, in the light of my bitterness, retrace accurately the growth of our affection. I remember only that he slowly schooled me in the labyrinths of his mind, unfolding a past as desolate as my own, until I found myself looking forward with avidity to our next meeting. He told me of his fear that he would rise at a concert, during a pianissimo, face as much of the audience as sat behind him, and bow, saying: "How do you do, odd fellows." He described how, in earlier years, he had admitted vices he did not possess, and how he had made his confessions ring true by promising to renounce these vices in the future. "I can distinguish between a baby's cry and the cry of a cat," he told me, "by noting whether the sound makes me unhappy. If it makes me unhappy, it is a baby's cry; for it restores by a correspondence too deep for analysis the years of my fatherhood," though he never, at any other time, spoke to me of either his marriage or an illicit union. And he would not have it that his indulgent ways of living sapped him of any essential vigour. "With the fed and clothed and comfortably bedded," he insisted, "there arise new terms of difficulty, remote parlour equivalents to the resistances which mute forbears summoned to meet the inexorable advance of glaciers." In his study of mental maladies, he said, he realized how many valleys he had passed through, and was sometimes astonished at his survival—yet he felt that he was permanently protected through having, on two different occasions, watched a human brain rot like a carcass in summer. "Thereafter one could never permit himself that complacency with madness which is at the roots of all madness, for he could not consider such decomposition of his own gifts as in any way an effective rebuke to other men."

He was erudite in a certain kind of despair. "Some years ago," he told me, "I dreamed that while I was repulsing a woman, in twilight, two terrifying shapes appeared at a door. I commanded them to leave, but they would not—and when I attempted to plead with them, I was so filled with dread that my voice became inaudible. Then of a sudden changing my tactics, I threw my arms about the woman and laughed at them—whereupon they and the dream were gone. I awoke to find myself repeating with exceptional solemnity, as though the words were a holy text, 'Love and humour can rescue me from my specific dangers. . . . Let this be remembered as the advice of an expert.' I have since followed the advice scrupulously by observing its contrary, as befits the interpretation of a dream. I have avoided charity and humour, which enable us to shed our profounder responsibilities. In permitting ourselves the weakness of doing good for others, by the simplicity of kindnesses we are blunted to the complex. And humour shies at all fundamental risk, making our burdens tolerable by a contrivance which reduces them to trivial proportions." He had turned rather, he said, to the rigours of loneliness: "We may produce a monster merely by stressing some aspects of our nature and suppressing others—and loneliness is to be welcomed precisely because it encourages such stressings and suppressions. Accordingly, I have lived in solitude. I had so well learned to protect myself that I found it necessary to invent ways of placing myself in jeopardy, lest the best muscles of my mind grow flabby." At one period, however, when his tests had become unbearable, he answered many advertisements, that he might receive mail daily.

"I have no memory of my parents," he told me one mild evening after we had walked through the busier sections of the city, and were seated on a deserted stretch of green overlooking the river. "I was raised by a guardian who at times was very brutal to me, and at other times would come to me in tears, asking my forgiveness. Shortly before I was of age, this silent and unstable man became dangerously ill. Thinking he was on his death-bed, he called me to him and confessed to squandering most of the fortune which he had held in trust for me. He recovered, but I made no mention of the matter to him. I took over the remainder of the estate soon afterwards, and was relieved to find that at least there was still enough for me to live on. Except for brief conversations on very unimportant subjects, there was henceforth a complete silence between us. I never reproached him—and through not accusing him, I robbed him of a defence. It was the one form of

163

retaliation left me." After a pause, he continued: "If you do not accuse a man for an unfairness he has done you, he will accuse himself—and since self-reproaches will go much deeper and be more accurately aimed than any attack from without, he will never forgive you. I was gratified to see this man, who now had no authority whatsoever over my resources, consume himself with an ineffectual vindictiveness. I believe that he practically withered away through hating me." And he went on to discuss the corrosiveness of the unavowed, telling me among other things an anecdote of an unbeliever he had known, with a pious wife. "He feared that she was praying for him—and indeed, at certain times of the day or night he seemed to feel the processes of her prayer. When she repeatedly denied that she prayed for him, and he had convinced himself that her piety would not permit her to mis-state the matter, he became certain that she was praying for him without herself knowing it. In the end, the intangibility of the situation drove him to such lengths of brooding that he struck the poor woman as she knelt beside her bed, and he then went mad fearing the wrath of a deity whose existence he denied."

"But you have suffered times wherein the thought of you was nauseous?" I pled with him, for it was exceptional solace, when his thinking touched my own at so many points, to find still further likenesses in our experience. "I believe I have spent my life in the realm of detestations," he answered me. "And occasionally, that the rules of conduct might grow simple and decisions come easy, I have deliberately sought the approval of people I despise. One cannot take such measures until he has been thoroughly disgruntled with his own limits. I understand now, that when undergoing strains upon my self-respect, I was greatly assisted by the prevalence of Hebrews, who unknowingly bore the brunt of my difficulties. Regardless of how humiliated I might feel, in my belittling of this race I took on dignity. In calling a man a Jew, with fury, I was assuaged—for here was a dishonour from which I was for ever saved. To denigrate him was to lift myself above him, not by the uneasy method of going off alone, but by the comforting inclusion of myself in a vast opposing band. So I should judge the presence of a discredited people very helpful to the thwarted and to those stung with a general rancour." Then taking up a stick, he began making figures in the dust. "Why, I was so thoroughly enmeshed that I would everywhere make the same representation of my dilemma, first an angle opening to the left (⌐), then an angle opening to the right ($\llcorner$), and then a line ($\_$) beneath the two, serving to join them; thus: $\underline{\,\sqcup\,}$. On noting that I had for weeks been drawing this form on the margins of newspapers, in the air, and even by running my eyes along the edges of buildings to translate other designs into this one, I realized how deep-seated was the conflict I had expressed thus graphically, and how constant my need to resolve it." As I said nothing, he added: "Yet through dividing oneself into parts, one will be exalted in moments of their sudden reunion. Distrust is but the preparation for certainty—and when doubters have ceased to doubt, in certainty they give no quarter."

He was competent at the piano, often devoting many consecutive hours to moody pieces, at other times preferring music in which there was much ingenuity. One evening when we were in his apartment, and he had interpreted an operatic score for me with unusual zest, after we had drunk somewhat, seeing that we were alone, and not liable to be interrupted, like youngsters we toyed with each other. A few days later, he invited me to live with him, which I did until the time when he proposed that we take a short trip together. On returning to the city, he suggested that I go straight to the apartment and that he would follow me shortly. But when I arrived there, I found that all his furniture had been removed during our absence. And on a window sill was a brief note from him containing money and explaining that he had vanished. Standing in the midst of this desolation, I recalled words he had said to me when we were last together in this room. "If there were some act," he had said slowly, "if there were some act, greatly degrading, I should go and commit this act, for the immoral alone have the true keenness of moral strivings. A thief is nearer to God than is any man of honour, because he is nearer to fear and nearer to the yearning not to steal. It is among the untroubled that virtue and religion perish." I understood now that when saying this to me, he had already decided to abandon me.

One tells himself: You are a clever fellow; you have talents; some women have liked to kiss you; you can, in various manners, battle. One tells himself: You are not fat, not generally abhorrent, you have had friends with whom there was satisfactory interchange. Not yet starving, not yet living in a hovel, not subject to the oppression of an alien conqueror, not greatly weakened by illness. One considers his assets, thus negatively, seeking to arrive at assurance by elimination. But there is good cause for uneasiness when one finds so late that he has accumulated nothing, that no material possession is his by the inertia of the law, and no person is bound to him by the habits born of long affection. Through being apprenticed to a shoe-maker one ultimately becomes a master, but there are no outward signs to mark the degrees of our particular discipline. If we, in periods of respite, had trained ourselves to deny God calmly, and even reverently, perhaps we could be assured of our continued stalwartness when under stress. That one should live in such a way that he had with him these three considerations daily: madness, the Faith, and death by his own hand! Still, on seeing the moon rise over the city, I do not think of death primarily, but of that Chinese poet, long dead, who wrote of drinking alone in the moonlight. Many pleasant schemes of existence have vanished, as such well-written documents from the past can testify. Henceforth, Genevieve, I will deserve you (he will deserve you, that is, if you will not hold against him the negligible shred of comfort he had got for himself recently by talking in two voices).

Purifyings by ritual, relief by the utterance of a formula, contrivances whereby, after so many sentences, the supplicant becomes a new man, denying such untoward yesterdays as are still recorded in the upbuilding of his tissues—I will not allow that things can be so erased. I will consider all past happenings as preserved in the present; and what is to be undone, will be undone only by our heaping a vast future upon it. I will permit myself no subterfuges of silence. I will not yield to the irresponsibilities of the Faith, which comforts by dismissing all variety of problems in the lump. For each particular difficulty, let there be a new statement. Let us not allow the evasiveness of one reply, worded in advance, for everything. I will not put myself among those blunt praisers of God who say "Glory to Allah" when there is an earthquake, "Glory to Allah" when there is a rose, "Glory to Allah" when they are fed, and "Glory to Allah" when Allah's glory itself is brought into question.

Does this bold man terrify you, Anthony? Then know that he went on a secret journey recently, arriving at nightfall, making his way unseen beyond a rainy town, creeping across a lawn, and peering into the windows of his former house, where he saw his former wife quite clearly. Then he stepped along a wall, among wet flowers, to the front door—and though he did not dare strike a match, he felt in the darkness where an embossed nameplate with his name upon it had once been fastened. There was a nameplate here, which he could not decipher, but as he counted the letters by touch he could tell for a certainty that neither his name, nor the name of his wife, was printed there. He returned to the town, and that he might leave as stealthily as he arrived, he boarded the next train from the dark side of the station.

IV. A story by John Neal

*Progress of curse. It is told indirectly by a story that he
writes about a lonely man and a dummy policeman.
Written around quotations from Blake. Particularly
towards the end, we see a close interweaving of the
story and the narrator's personal situation.*

Sept. 25

My dear,

All day I have been walking the streets in mild
despair. In the late afternoon I sat on a bench in
one of the small parks, and watched the sun sink.
He too, in this mid-September weather, is mild and
a little weary. His long debauch of summer has
weakened him but I, except for a few miraculous
hours not many months past, have known no strong
passions to be weak from. Oh, half of my soul,
animae dimidium meae as our bleary-eyed old Horace put it, let your affection for me do what my
affection for myself could never do: let it lead you
to forgive this indiscreet wailing. Without you to
hear me, I have no one. Of all these millions of
people, the single one who has shown me a spark
of recognition is a wooden policeman in front of a
cigar store nearby, a dummy if there ever was one.
He and I are akin, for his waxen dignity, his benign

171

officialdom, is as eternal, as hopelessly inalterable, as my mild despair.

But you see what unhealthy preoccupations I have fallen into. Lamp posts, street cars, gutters have characters for me, when people do not. And as a consequence, I cannot continue my work. I am subdued, and a little dazed. My uprooting has not given me the assistance we thought it would. So you must not delay much longer. For if an occasional quick breath of hope raises this burden of dismalness that is upon me, it is because I dare expect you. Yet I can promise you nothing, nothing but the abject tributes of one who loves you "like the little bird that picks up crumbs around the door," if I may quote again a passage from Blake which you have heard me quote so often. I have stood before the glass and told myself: "What claims do you have upon her? By what right could you ask her to come here?" If one must expect much to get a little, how can I encourage you to join me? For if attainments fall short of ambitions, and I dare look forward to nothing, what a ghastly result we have after the subtraction!

Yesterday, in spite of my loathing, I forced myself to work at the twelfth chapter, where my hero clearly sees the implications of his character converging upon him. The sort of life he has constructed is becoming inexorably apparent to him. He is lonely, my dear, even as lonely as I—and his loneliness will undo him. He has made himself a Mole, to learn what Eagles cannot imagine. A writer can, out of the depths of himself, invent but one new aspect of vice; no wonder that he prizes it greatly and dignifies it by having it cause the destruction of his hero. So in my behalf, the poor devil must suffer. We have allowed him to retain a kind of sullen optimism, an ill-natured praise of God, but I would not put any faith in the chances of either himself or his author.

Oct. 12

My dear,

If you have not received any letters from me for a couple of weeks, it is not because I have not written to you. No day has passed in which I have not devoted many hours to you. But I have always become ashamed of my complainings, and have destroyed them. Will she ever have us, I have warned myself, if we go on discouraging her with our self-doubts? I thank you that you have not scolded me for my silence. I worked doggedly all day today, despite the repugnance of the task, and succeeded in

173

piling up eight thousand more sluggish words. (Eight thousand more, by count. Remember our Blake: "Bring out number weight & measure in a year of dearth." He knew this curse, through knowing so well the corresponding privilege:

"Every time less than a pulsation of the artery
  Is equal in its period & value to Six Thousand
    Years,
  For in this Period the Poet's Work is Done, and
    all the Great
  Events of Time start forth & are conceiv'd in such
    a Period:
  Within a Moment, a Pulsation of the Artery."

I read him often now, our Blake. I marvel that he could invent such "Giant forms" as never were, yet could know beyond hesitancy how each one looked and how each one would have spoken. It is only in my letters to you that I am fluent—but these, in sheer self-protection, I must repeatedly destroy. My genius resides in loving you abjectly.)

Still, there are compensations. For I was exhausted, and I swear that I should never touch this desolate work again were it not that I must earn you, that I must make some visible thing which entitles me to you. I was exhausted, until my very tissues drooped with nausea. I fled from my room into the crisp fall air, hoping only for a physical recovery. But the wind attacked me, and I walked furiously, tingling. And of a sudden I understood that something more than mere bodily exaltation was upon me. "What does the damned book matter," I cried, "when she will soon be here to comfort me!" I felt again the prodigal ambitions of those days when you talked with me and pictured for me the future of both of us. You, I understood, would make my work prosper. And I felt so very good that on the way back to my room I could not resist one happy wink at my friend, the dummy policeman. Indeed, I did more than that. I noticed that on his pedestal he bore a message recommending a certain brand of cigar. I immediately entered his store and bought one. It was a wretched cigar, and as you know I don't care much for even good cigars, but I played fair, and smoked that cigar to the dregs.

"Dear Mother, dear Mother, the Church is cold,
But the Ale-house is healthy & pleasant & warm,"

I sang to myself, the little vagabond did sing—for at the thought of you he had left the gloomy Church of his recalcitrant novel, to sit in the cozy Ale-house of his love. I did not mind my previous miserableness, since its cure was so thorough. And I was shamelessly indebted to you. If one has great distinctness, he will search long before he finds in another that sweet combination of traits which forms his precise complement—and if he finds her, is it not reasonable that he should think of her unceasingly? Oh, do not mistake me. In speaking of my distinctness, I do not hint at exceptional abilities. A man would be distinct with noses for ears. I mean simply that for each lack in me, you brought the corresponding fulness; that wherever I was in need, you had the fitting kind of charity. Thirst is a delight where there is water; where food is plentiful, hunger is a luxury. I did not now regret my particular ills, since they turned me with such avidity to you as the cure for them. You recall, in *Jerusalem*, the passage on Mary's love which we enjoyed so greatly, and how you would laugh when I insisted that with us the sexes should be reversed—me Mary, and you Joseph:

"Then Mary burst forth into a Song: she flowed like
   a River of
Many Streams in the arms of Joseph & gave forth
   her tears of joy
Like many waters, and Emanating into gardens
   and palaces upon

Euphrates, & to forests & floods & animals wild &
   tame from
Gihon to Hiddekel, & to corn fields & villages &
   inhabitants
Upon Pison & Arnon & Jordan . . ."

I felt this expansiveness of Mary. I felt as though
I were pouring forth bounty—is that not funny,
when I was silent even, had not even one sentence
to offer, could show nothing more ambitious than my
gratitude to you?

                                        Nov. 7
My dear,
   It would be a relief for me to think that for once
I can write you about something other than myself;
and I should be thankful for this respite were it not
caused by the pressure of a topic equally repellent.
How, *animae dimidium meae*, could you have confessed to me so casually that you found your interest
in Blake waning? You still *perceive* his excellence,
you tell me, but it no longer matters whether he is
excellent or not. Has he himself not obliquely re-
futed you when, in his *Marriage of Heaven and
Hell*, he reminds us: "Truth can never be told so as

to be understood, and not be believ'd"? If his excellence has ceased to matter, then you have ceased to perceive it—and where am I to turn, who realize only too well that the very foundations of our union rest upon Blake? If there was one event of great import in my life, it was the day in Altmann's meadow when we read *The Everlasting Gospel*, with its sublime doggerel so helpful to us in our uncertainties at that time. For it enwrapped our humble desires in a gorgeous vocabulary, making us feel that not merely you and I, but all Mankind and Womanhood, were on that day approaching each other. We were encouraged to scorn a law "writ with Curses from Pole to Pole," were told that God himself is no more than man, and that "Mary was found in Adulterous bed."

> "But this, O Lord, this was my Sin
> When first I let these devils in:
> In dark pretence to Chastity
> Blaspheming Love, blaspheming thee."

You, to my astonishment, paused to repeat these lines. I was terrified at your sudden lewd promise, stated thus with the authority of a great poet, and I myself begged you to put me away until I should make myself more worthy of you.

So consider, my dear, how much you would take from us by this moody heresy. Let us admit no "idiot Questioner" in matters of such great moment to our relationship. And you should not protest at my homage. How could you in any way feel yourself "absurd" when I write you as I do? You should find it only natural that I praise you diligently; you should receive me amply, and think no further.

Yet I have been more disciplined than you would suspect. I have spared you all the letters I wrote you following the announcement of your delay. I had bought tickets for the opera, which I could ill afford; but that I might not be there wholly without you, I did not turn back the ticket to the seat which you would have occupied. Thus by my subterfuge, in your very absence you were somehow with me. "The weak in courage is strong in cunning"—and I have contrived many tricks of thinking to help bear me up.

How pleasant, after the strained hours I had spent recently in the coercing of my story, to place myself at the disposal of a master, to let him dictate when there should be risings and when subsidences. I assisted him—and together we mounted to assertion, capped by kettledrums. And as another evidence of my cunning, I left the theatre before the close of the performance, I went away while the violins were repeating a design in unison, ever more softly, and the stage gradually darkened, suggesting the submerged castle of a fish bowl and the mighty distances discoverable there by peering. I left before the end that I might carry away the sense of the opera's continuing—and for several hours afterwards it seemed as though that vast battle were still in progress. I went from opera sounds to street sounds, but the imperiousness of the music was still strong in me, and every casual noise was translated into the perfect note most like it. Thus the discordant city sang melodically and contrapuntally. Were I a charitable deity, looking down upon what was there myself, if I were such a deity, observing that hollow replica, and concerned with nothing but his particular respite, I should have said: "Strike him down—let him at this moment cease." And if there is disloyalty to you in such a thought, take it as the one sign I will give you of my discouragement at your delay. Oh, I am tired—tired of trying to deserve you, tired of writing you so constantly and so unmanfully. May you come soon, to repair all this—may you come, that I may nestle against you, and repeat then with comfort:

"Ah! gentle may I lay me down and gentle rest my
   head,
And gentle sleep the sleep of death, and gentle hear
   the voice
Of him that walketh in the garden in the evening
   time."

                                        Jan. 19
   Please do not hold it against me that I was so long
in answering you. You will understand me when I
say that I had to wait for a little competence. I had
to find such a way of writing you that I should not
pain you either by vindictiveness or by too greatly
appealing to your pity. I could not write to wish you
well until not only my words, but the man writing
these words in his empty room, could wish you well.
And in all fairness, I must agree with you as to the
wisdom of your choice. I did not hold out a very en-
couraging future to you.
   "Damn braces. Bless relaxes." Yet I will not
equip myself against you by venom. I will tell myself always that you were sweet, and thus I shall
remain unfortified. For if I hated you now, how
could I continue to love you in the past—and for me
not to love you in the past would be an impoverish-

ment beyond endurance. Oh yes, I will not deny that
for some weeks the Undersigned has been a "Male
Form howling in Jealousy," his Emanation torn
from him. He "furious refuses to repose." He has
the disconcerting documents at his fingertips, recalls
that "the nakedness of woman is the work of God,"
that "Women, the comforters of Men, become their
Tormentors & Punishers," nor can he dismiss the
recollection of a lovely twilight when, after the two
of them had walked for many miles, and had eaten
the supper he carried in his knapsack, they nestled
together under birch-trees. He needs but imagine another in his place, and the picture is circumstantial
enough. "Dip him in the river who loves water." Yet
not Blake, but you, have taught me not to invite
disaster.

"The Hermaphroditic Condensations are divided by
　　the Knife,
　The obdurate Forms are cut asunder by Jealousy
　　and Pity."

Of jealousy I have spoken. I know that in jealousy
the world is lost. Yet jealousy is but incidental to
deep single love; it is the risk, not the essence; and
if the world is lost in jealousy, in deep single love
the world may be well lost. The possibilities of de-

light were worth the eventualities of torture. As for pity, though there is a division in pity, and though I had sworn not to ask for pity, I shall be content with pity. I shall tell myself that you have not ceased to worry for me. Thus I shall relinquish a great deal that I may salvage a little, for one should not try to save too much in a fire. Oh, I am caught in the "mind-forg'd manacles," though in this case they are not the manacles of reason, but the manacles of a relentless, unreasoning memory.

I know of a man who, in a moment of blind self-interest that undid its own purposes, had sent away a lovely woman. Needing money, he had suggested sullenly that she procure some as best she was able, yet there had been much delicacy in his possession of her. She left the room without reproaching him, but he never saw her again thereafter—and with each succeeding month he understood more bitterly the destitution he had brought upon himself. He found that she alone had upheld him, for there was no pliancy in him that had not come from sources within this woman. He remembered how they had crept together, with the city roaring about them like a monster; how he had felt the warmth of her while she slept, as though they alone were spared from a cataclysm, as though all mankind, torn by madness, were fleeing from danger, while they lay safely in sweet segregation, enclosed in the Ark of their four walls, and the torrents of the metropolis pounded outside their windows. But the room had since become barren of her—so he grew humble, he grew really pitiable, and I was very sorry for him, particularly as I saw a feeling of strangeness and loneliness come over him, and I knew that by his very need of companionship he drove people from him. There seemed no way of rescuing him, for if some one spoke to him easily, he would promptly whisper to himself, "See, the man felt no strain in addressing me," and in thinking such thoughts he would betray them to the speaker, who then felt uneasy, and shied away at an excessive leaping-up of gladness. Let us hope, my dear, that I do not, in my own way, gradually lapse into this man's strangeness—but I fear lest all that smiled readily in me has been taken from me.

I enclose, along with my felicitations, my unfinished manuscript. What cause could I have to plague myself with it further? It was meant purely to earn me certain privileges which are no longer available. With this I say good-bye. And that you may not think me wholly alone, I say good-bye also in behalf of the wooden policeman, who must know something about you since he has stared his paint-stare directly into my eyes. I shall write you no further. I have not the slightest notion what I shall do next. I shall vaguely advance—and perhaps, by the subterfuges of the cowardly cunning, I shall have nothing more real than the wooden man for my grotesque crony, as I go towards the tangled and uncharted, into

> "Realms
> Of terror & mild moony lustre, in soft sexual delu-
> sions
> Of varied beauty to delight the wanderer and repose
> His burning thirst and freezing hunger!"

Henceforth I shall at best be one of those "that live a pestilence and die a meteor and are no more."

March 8

To my dear dead Mistress,

I did, it is true, promise never to write you again. But surely you will allow me the harmless pleasure of a make-believe correspondence, writing letters you never receive, and answering letters you never sent.

Well, it has not been so painful as I had feared,

this being deprived of Emanation, and cursed by Selfhood. With the unfinished manuscript I sent you, the bafflements of fiction have ceased, and now I roam about devoid of any such grave responsibilities. One tramps streets of dirty, half-melted snow, observing the minor incidents of traffic. In sitting among audiences, and looking in the same direction with them, one feels not wholly outcast. I read but seldom, even Blake I read but seldom. The Ariel-like songs run through my head occasionally, but I am not, at this time, so greatly attracted to his mythological pieces, with their clangorous forge-music, "uttered with Hammer & Anvil," their cosmic lamentations, their accounts of vast Beings' wombs raped vastly, their torrents, violent awakings, earthquakes, rebirths. Such fountainheads of poetry are not wholly germane to my chief problems at present.

I have heard of people who found it impossible to prevent themselves from counting numbers, and continued long into the night, in anguish, piling up their involuntary sums. Similarly with me, the idea of the dummy policeman has come to be troublesome. Perhaps I should take a room in some other section of the city. For this absurd figure stands too prominently in my path. With a life so uneventful as mine, it becomes too much of an event for me to pass him. And even while sitting in my room, as let us say on some snowy night when I have no intention of going out, I keep thinking of him on the street below, with stolidly upraised hand, the sleet curving about his pedestal. There is nothing particularly unpleasant in the thought of him except its constancy. And I can assure you: he is so unchanging, that to think of him repeatedly is to feel the mind inexorably rigid. To consider him against one's wishes is like maintaining a constant muscular tension. So you may, before long, find me in retreat from this grotesque danger. If he continues to claim more of my attention, I shall certainly take a room in another section of the city.

March 28

My dear dead Mistress,

One reason the figure has taken such a hold upon me is that I have had little opportunity to bury its effects beneath more natural kinds of relationship. Seeing a child in a carriage, I took advantage of its ignorance to wheedle a smile from it—and the mother came near me hurriedly, meaning no insult, but clearly nervous at finding me so close to something she thought precious. A sweet woman once

187

took delight in the touch of me, and I sat in many ordinary places conversing with strangers readily enough, and people did not think it odd—but now I can approach no human thing without remarkableness.

Two young men recently sat on the same bench with me in the park. They seemed like students, and from their conversation I knew that their studies were of great import to them. Thus I felt I could tell them things which might somewhat engross them; but when I spoke, though I quoted good authors in order to make my equipment apparent to them in my opening sentences, they showed clearly that they resented my intrusion. The far one uncrossed his legs, so I knew that the boys would leave me as soon as possible. I talked hastily to them about the vicious circle, calling it both "vicious circle" and *circulus vitiosus*, using the Latin that they might know me for no ordinary man on a park bench, and the English lest they might not understand the Latin. "I am in a vicious circle," I said in haste, for they were growing shifty. There are accounts of such vicious circles in folk-lore, I explained to them, as stories of a once handsome prince locked up in a repellent form. "These are stories of the vicious circle," I told them, "for the Prince will not be freed until the love of a beautiful woman has freed him—and how, short of magic, can a beautiful woman love him until his true form is revealed?" But I had made them very uncomfortable, so I turned abruptly and went away from them. Surely they smiled to each other behind my back; yet had they made friends with me simply as an oddity, and admitted me into their lives on any terms, if only as a king might keep a dwarf or a parrot, I should gradually have been reclaimed. Of this I am certain.

April 3

My dear dead Mistress,

I am a little frightened today, for the rigidity of my existence is unquestionably beginning to tell against me. If one were to make his hand into a fist so tightly clenched that the whole arm trembled, and were to translate this feeling to mental things, he could imagine somewhat how my mind is. It is as though my mind had muscles, and these muscles would not relax. The steadiness of my preoccupation causes this feeling of muscles under tension. It is as though the pulpy substance of the brain were turning into muscle, and these muscles were straining to tear apart their own tissues. This feeling is clearly the result of a tension caused by a changeless image which I cannot dismiss. But just as the eye accommodates itself to blinding lights, or the skin gradually learns to withstand heat of great intensity, I could probably make myself sufficiently at home under this discipline, did I not have a fear that its severity is growing. I had become competent enough—but today, when I passed my policeman, a quick impulse seized me, and before I knew what I was doing, I had spoken to the policeman. I wish I had not done this—and I should not have done it had I been aware of the temptation in advance. Just as though he were alive, I smiled at him and spoke. I was passing directly in front of him when, to my astonishment, I heard myself saying, "Hello, Joe." I could have done the same under happier circumstances, but the meaning would not have been the same. It is quite natural to address inanimate things—it is no more foolish than confiding secrets to a dog. But as I looked about apprehensively, I saw that a woman had observed me. She was pretty, and insolent, and was watching me intently. There was no kindness in her eyes, nothing but cold curiosity. Her eyes, my dear, passed a terrible judgment upon me. And to escape her judgment, I repeated my greeting, this time leaning back, squinting, and waving my hand, as though I had been speaking to some one in the recesses of the store—but now I noticed that the clerk inside, with a bewildered moonface, was staring at me glumly. I am now bending beneath eyes, the wooden eyes of the policeman, the cold curious eyes of the woman, and the glum eyes of the clerk inside the store.

April 7

To my dear, dead Mistress,

My life is a funnel—and with each day I am squeezed farther into its narrow end. This morning, with a strange assurance, I leapt from my bed, dressed, and hurried down to the street, just that I might pass the policeman and show myself that I could pass him without speaking. I did pass him without speaking, without even a desire to speak to him. But when I had returned to my room, a voice said to me, "Could you pass him again without speaking?" So I went down and passed him again. Five times today I have passed the policeman, to convince myself that I need not speak to him as I pass him; but each time, as I go back to my room, the doubt returns.

Now, it has occurred to me, why should I not

speak to the policeman? I have been plagued by
the conviction that I should not speak to him—and
the obvious way of overcoming that is to let oneself
speak to him. I had made a new temptation by making a new crime—and I shall remove them both at
once. Hereafter, if I happen to desire to address the
dummy, I shall do so. I shall speak to him as often
as I please. And as a precaution against cold curious
stares of unsympathetic women, I shall speak to him
covertly, from the corner of my mouth, behind my
handkerchief, or by hiding my mouth with my hand
as though I were scratching my nose.

Memorandum: Rules to Self: If a person whistles
or calls, give no evidence of hearing. The signal
was not intended for you. If children begin shouting, do not quicken your pace. The shouting has to
do with some game of theirs. You are dressed like
every other man that passes along these streets. If
strangers in the city stop to ask you directions, act
as though you spoke another language and did not
understand them. You know by now that when they
ask you questions, your knowledge of the commonest
streets will vanish from your memory. So avoid embarrassment by acting as though you could not un-

derstand them. Never stop beside some one who is looking in a shop window, if he is alone. For you know how it irritates you when you are standing alone looking in a shop window and some one stops beside you and begins looking at the same things. If you decide to go the other way, try to remember not to turn suddenly—for likely as not there will be some one behind you, and his face will be thrust directly into yours.

April 8

My dear Mistress,

No, you are not dead. Praise God, you are not dead. When I finally need to do so, I can really write to you, can actually mail one of these letters to you. So you may soon be hearing from me in reality, for I may need your help, I may have to call upon you to end a certain process. Today it seemed that the policeman actually acknowledged me in passing. I know that the policeman did not speak to me. It was probably some chance street-sound that was interpreted, by my tired body, as a voice coming from him. And it was probably a mere quiver of my eyelids which made me imagine for a moment that his lips moved. Besides, any rigid thing, if watched intently, will seem to stir. Who has not, on observing a statue or a corpse, seen the breast heave in respiration? When the dummy seemed to stir for a moment I was not frightened. But a second later, apprehension came over me. I looked about— and as I had feared, the cold curious woman was eyeing me, and passing the same judgment upon me. Oh, I am very tired. I should like to fall into a deep sleep, and on awaking, find every single thing around me altogether different.

I said that I could write you? On the contrary, I must not think of writing you. Probably it was the weakness of these make-believe letters that first started me on my course into the funnel. I must put myself under severer rules. I must deny myself all these little subterfuges which pamper me. This is the last word that passes between us.

V. "In partial recapitulation"

A selective, and amplified, review of his life.

T HERE are, underlying the Church, many ingenious heresies so thoroughly silenced by the
sword that they survive only in the refutations of
the faithful. There are subtle schemes deriving the
best of human insight from Cain, or centering salvation upon the snake, or lauding the act of Judas
Iscariot which procured for uneasy mankind a God
as scapegoat. To look back upon them is to consider
a wealth of antinomian enterprise expended in ways
which seem excessive, troublesome, and unnecessary,
their gratuity being surpassed only by the same qualities among the orthodox. But let one not be misled
into thinking that the heresies have perished. They
rise anew, changing their terms each time, to stand
against the new terms of the Faith, squarely. Their
doctrines need not be handed down jealously from
generation to generation, but may be neglected without risk of loss. Our Bulgars require but the spirit of
their cause, a spirit which takes form by the form of

the current dogmas, knowing what not to accept by noting what is accepted. Oh, lepers of mankind; gutter-rats; printers in the sewers; you the pale with prison pallor; the discredited, the unprosperous, you who can make no answer, for your voices are drowned by the roar of the believers (they need not refute you, they need but restate to one another all that they had already said, humiliating you by thinking of their own plans and singing among themselves); you the worthless, the salt-smugglers, the bringers of illicit drugs to comfort the unhappy to whom the moneyed would permit not even chemical relief; you the thieves, who outrageously disturb the security of the privileged; you the insidious promoters of subversive doctrines which would allow the starved to nibble somewhat at the world's plethoric stores; you who are gnawed by misgivings, who would gladly renounce your own bitter birthright, gladly take your place among the exclusive, scorning your old companions, turning from oppressed to oppressors (and thus, precisely in your state of rebellion you uphold their systems, considering your insight wickedness, yourself admitting your degradation, yearning for acceptance by those very persons against whom you are pitted)—oh, you in every manner unequipped, you the deprived of logic, the improvident, the indolent who cannot strive for such crooked kinds of happiness as those in authority would force upon you—all you disheartened, discountenanced, disorganized—I salute you, for if there is to be a remedy, this remedy will come because you have made it imperative.

Some years ago, in this very city, I stepped lightly through a door leading to the street—and as I walked vigorously away, triply elated with liquor, a sense of futurity, and the briskness of the autumn weather, I felt no quarrel with anything this city stands for. Why should I complain at the rules of a contest in which I seemed likely to do well? True, I had doubts about the standards by which achievement would be rated, but I felt that one should first be successful by the criteria of other men before setting up criteria of his own. Let him make money, that is, before railing against wealth; let him get reputation before calling all reputation worthless; whatever he would renounce, let him first acquire it in ample quantities, that he become immune to hecklers. The weather, as I have said, was crisp, and I was young and slightly drunken, and still buoyed up by the good outcome of some financial dealing, and I smiled negligently at a woman, not needing her since a woman even then was awaiting me. I could regret a plague in India, or sigh that some men went hungry, but I was prepared to take all this with resignation, feeling that our fate is but the tossing of a coin, and relieved that I happened to be on the favourable side of the toss. Entering another building, I rode to a high floor—for one must go up into high places to be tempted—and from here I surveyed the jumble of the city. Ah, Anthony, perhaps I have since been better than I thought. For did I not put every action beneath questioning? Though I may too often have ended in a sanction, I can assure you that the question was what mattered. I devoted my best efforts, not to making myself more effective in some given purpose, but to a weighing of this purpose. If I spoke much of fitness, and seemed at times too shrewd in profiting by the simplicity of Genevieve, I swear that this was but a flare-up before extinction, as men do not study folkways until these folkways are passing. At great inconvenience I maintained the integrity of my character, often choosing to grow sullen where I might have dismissed a dilemma by laughter—laughter, which leaves us untried, which is a stifler in the interests of comfort, surrendering in advance, renouncing prior to excess, enabling a man to avoid the ultimate implications of his wishes. I put Genevieve from me, not because our relationship was faulty, but because I had to put some dear thing from me. And if I showed great adulation of prosperity, be it prosperity in matters of health, money, or affection, I did so because I felt great prosperity necessary to equip the body for the strain of investigation and possible insight.

I did things. At the time of doing them I told you why I did them. And now, if I assert that I did them for other reasons, by what authority can you say that I was then correct in my analysis and am wrong now? You must hear me out, when I can observe my course through a considerable stretch of time, can verify and correct earlier tentative calculations, can better know what I was making for, by seeing what I have come to. Consider with what difficulty one would go about it to attain something he very much desired. Add to these obstacles the exceptional burdens of my particular character. Add further that I could think of no specific end towards which I would undividedly strive or the attainment of which would give me sound satisfaction. And thus you see how I was buried, three layers deep. If one questions the beliefs of other men without having well-grounded beliefs of his own, he will find himself deficient by any scale of measurements.

Though no one would choose failure, we may yet maintain that failure is a choice, since one may persist in attitudes which make his failure inevitable. Yet, I have fondly pictured groups of citizens coming to reward me, entering my room while a band plays in the street below, and announcing, "The time is over," thereupon presenting me with testimonials of their respect and explaining that they have picked me for some minor office. I should work hard, I should justify their confidence fully, I have told myself—yet I have never made the appropriate efforts which would prepare me for distinctions of the sort. Place a man among these streets, instruct him to choose some act which puts a strain upon his temper. What work will he perform here, if it is work in the absolute, and not the accidental matter of flunkeying to an employer? If he does not mean by work the earning of a little money through assisting in a superior's blind purposes, but the straining of his resources, what manner of living must he choose? What indeed but risk, risk of imprisonment, of disease, of ridicule? How be called muscular if you did not prefer the sewers and rat-holes of the metropolis? If you are able in ways that bring you no advantage, would you admit yourself unable? Choose rather the dignity of a savage chieftain, which coexists with vermin. What did Alter Ego say? "There are many kinds of effort," he said, "which people without spirit and without physical enterprise are best equipped for, just as cockroaches are more likely than tigers to flourish in sinks." While I hesitated, buyers and sellers had faith—and though their faith is such that it ultimately brings the world to hell, it will have brought them privilege and power in the interim. Die as a mangled wasp dies—its body hunched, its wings futile, but its sting groping viciously for its tormentor. Prowling about the wharves, I have ministered to unclean men, for in this there was some ghastly decency, something beyond mere safety.

Oh, there is a revolutionary unction. There are the blasts of the well fed and well entrenched, comfortably summoning the people to rebel, calling for the destruction of a system built for bankers, and all the while they are bolstered up with stipends from the bankers. They are the bankers' conscience—and in proportion as the bankers gain further questionable wealth, so will these consciences of bankers be generously treated. But note that they make their protests more picturesque than malicious, and can be kept about the house like castrated lion whelps, providing a certain edge of excitement but no serious danger. Are they fostering defiance, or milking a cow?

Let me, in partial recapitulation, recall that, all my life, I chose unerringly. How, at the farmhouse, I went alone to the stables, that you might walk with the girl by the river; how I procured for you the part as Alcaeus and for Florence the part of Mary, thus enabling you to transfer these flattering rôles into your relations with each other; how I schemed to my detriment in the matter of keys; how, on the island, I industriously made myself repugnant; how, when I had fled and had earned modest distinctions, I refused to please myself with them, but still lamented and imprecated as though I were generally looked down upon; how I was careful to eschew any permanent elation at Florence's return; how I vilified a group that had befriended me; how I saw to it that Genevieve, who could comfort me, was driven from me; and how, though I anticipated the results, I permitted Alter Ego to understand my dependence upon him, until he vanished. Know me, Anthony, as a man whose purpose never wavered. Through living under difficulty, one learns the mode of thinking, feeling, and acting best suited to cope with difficulty. No wonder he prizes a discovery which he has made at so great inconvenience to himself, and will not relinquish it but calls upon it to maintain precisely those adversities which it was at first designed to remedy.

Let us consider the matter in this wise: Take as a hypothetical case John Neal, a somewhat quarrelsome fellow who was ingenious in the cultivation of an illness not yet completely catalogued. I, had I met him, could have made proper allowances for him; but others had no cause to do so, especially as he was without authority, and kowtowings on their part would have gone unrewarded. Where they might have felt nothing, he forced them to resent him a little; and when he had made them resent him a little, he lay awake calling for their forgiveness, calling so frankly, so unstintingly, that by morning the cycle of contrition had run its course, and on next seeing them and finding them still resentful despite his unavowed beseechments, he was annoyed, and sought to punish them for their uncharitableness, thereby adding to their resentment. Subsequently, as the result of this process, our John Neal was without cronies. And at this point he prayed, calling upon that Name which heretofore had been for him an oath.

He prayed under no mean circumstances. For he had left the city, had gone to a little hut on a hilltop, and was living there alone, feared by the children of the nearby village though I can assure you that he would not have harmed them. A stifling August twilight had been converted, by sudden clouds, into a blackness without direction. A storm of vast proportions had let loose against the hut, which shook, for it was a little Ark, and outside was such a chaos as beat upon the Ark. That night a battle was waged. There were two storms that night, one at the roof, the other in a lone man's brain. I believe he knew the fertility of madness, the inestimable range of madness. Alone in his Ark he cried out, calling for his former friends as though they could ride upon the storm. Suddenly the door was wrenched open—he leapt forward, "I greet you, damned demons!" he shouted, then closed the door hastily, shutting out the rain-laden wind, and leaving nothingness within. Mountains of thunder were piled up and toppled. The lightning, which made a licking sound, was crowded by new flashes. And all the while he called down violence upon him, demanding greater and greater extravagance of the elements. In the morning, when this intense effort had subsided, and the sun, as seen from the hilltop, rolled above a sea of mist, he walked beneath dripping trees, across a field mowed recently, down to a little

lake which lay like glass beneath pink mist. Here
he found nine cranes, pure white, their great whiteness making their silence deeper silence. He approached them with caution, with no abruptness
of movement, for their timidity was multiplied by
their number, all being sensitive to the misgivings of
each. Eventually they arose, and with adjustments
of the group they disappeared above the trees. Thus,
after fury came white gentleness, and he understood
that a sign had been vouchsafed him. He knelt,
while love poured from him, or poured into him
from all outward things—and to his vast astonishment, he heard words of prayer issuing like missiles
from his lips. For a manner of understanding, un-
sought for, had blossomed within him.

With each moment the universe is new created,
each succeeding tick of time presenting the same
alternatives: Will all life vanish in oblivion or
will it be divinely prodded to continue into one further modicum of future? The following moment of
existence comes; the universe still flourishes, not revealing in its magnificence that it has been spared
by a mere choice between God's acquiescence and
His refusal—whereat again there is the risk: Will
all life be sustained, or will it lapse? God the Crea-
tor as God the Eternal Re-creator, with the universe

suspended by a thread of prayer rising from human lips. If that day comes when all humanity is busied with its prosperity in human terms, and the miraculous thread of prayer is broken, then will our ingratitude have snapped the continuity of existence. In ages of dwindling piety, let adept worshippers keep long vigil, lest there arise a fatal moment of lapse when no thread of prayer joins us to our vital sources and the props and underpinnings of the universe are thus removed. Of those few earnest men scattered across the world, when all but one have fallen in exhaustion and are sleeping, upon the shoulders of this one alone is born the full weight of universal life. So it is good that some men are scorned by their fellows and made to feel homeless among them, since these outcasts are, through their sheer worldly disabilities, vowed to graver matters and could not, even if they would, prevent themselves from pouring forth their neglected love upon a formidable Father. By their very inadequacy they are shielded, being led back to God if only through their incompetence at betraying Him. So we may say that a man's sufferings are not unused if they but bring him to extremities—and by lone anguish on a hilltop, while storms tear at the walls of a house and the walls of a human mind, snug homes in valleys are kept secure. Those who were crucified were but erecting mountains of prayer, masses to carry beyond the subsequent moment and serve perhaps through centuries of silence.

Then John Neal, in choosing difficulty, was not acting without purpose? In his lying awake there was a preparation, in his selecting of misfortune an apprenticeship? Only those persons of pale desire are balked, and if they tell you how earnest and continuous are their hopes, talk with them a little further, until you see how soundly they sleep, how without discipline they glut themselves, how they do not compel themselves to walk at night in a bitter wind, how they do not take lighted matches and burn themselves for having made a faulty rejoinder, how they do not grow thin with study and admonitions. Thus they will reveal the falsity of their assertions by the flaccidness of their living. So I will not agree that this John Neal was denied what he desired. Throughout the tight continuum of the universe, what uncomplemented thing is possible? Need and fulfilment are one, as bursting cotyledons and laden stock are one, germination and fruition being aspects of a single happening. That which causes cannot act without that which is caused, whereby the prior is evoked by its consequences. The doing, the need of doing, and the done are indistinguishable. If some fulfilment of importance is to be granted us, this fulfilment is foreshadowed as a need. A yearning is but the premonition of an end. Seeing the ground thirsty, the leaves parched, dust-covered, drooping, the brooks sunk beneath their pebbles, we see the origins of a downpour. There is no cry for rain in a desert; there is a cry for rain where storms are brewing. Our complaints are the adumbration of a coming proficiency; in greatly suffering a need we but sense the earliest evidences of a fulfilment; I would not say that those who call out are answered —I would say, rather, that those destined to be answered must call out.

Thus documented, John Neal loved all mankind and prayed? On the contrary, he went to no hilltop, he shouted against no storm, he invited neither friends nor demons to ride Valkyrie-like. But sitting in his room, in this inexorable city, he said, rather: "Watch the mind, as you would eye a mean dog. Wait. Die as a mangled wasp dies." He constructed for himself a story, picturing himself as gentle, and imagining Genevieve as a woman who had deserted him (which was not difficult to imagine, for he had called her so often in his thoughts, that she seemed cruel in refusing to answer). But the sanction of no vast mythology was permitted him.

VI. "Testamentum Meum"

WOULD liken God to a little mouse, since the differences are obvious—whereas in likening God to the day, we obscure his splendour by suggesting the splendour of sunlight.

if one must seek solace, let it be in the cultivation of some power.

there were marked aspects of himself which Alter Ego would have greatly preferred to abandon—and on finding the same aspects in me, he quasi-abandoned them by abandoning me.

the liver gnawed by vultures, though you brought fire to no one.

madness, travel, drugs, the Faith, death by one's own hand.

to guard against prayer, particularly that secular form of prayer which is ambition. An act is but the simulacrum of a deeper act, a disguised way of coming into port, of feasting after hunger, which is the essential process of the universe. And in too greatly desiring some specific thing, either in prayer or in the strivings of the ambitious, we forget the metaphorical quality of all desires. The universe is Cause and Effect in one, Command and Obedience in one, Need and Fulfilment in one. Throughout eternity there is hunger in the fact that the universe *needs to be*, and appeasement in the fact that the universe *is*.

there is an eye, firm as the eye of the newly dead. When I am alone, this eye inspects me.

you cannot renounce, for none but the rich dare speak in praise of poverty.

have said: This is the day. There will be some sign, or more than a sign, a clear alteration. Today some thing has been changed to meet my needs. And if night falls without this new thing's becoming apparent, then the event was a letter written at a distance and started on its way but not yet delivered; or a decision reached by some one who has still to act upon it; or if the relief is to come wholly from within me, the process is even now at work, but has revealed its presence before revealing its nature.

if they cannot have religion, they should have lotteries.

speech being a mode of conduct, he converted his faulty living into eloquence. Then should any like his diction, they would indirectly have sanctioned his habits.

can conceive of two men, one rebellious, without compromise—the other given to half-measures. This second man, by his yieldings and flunkeyings, gets himself some modicum of independence—but the more thoroughgoing man has been too often routed in the interim: it is he who, to exist, must court favour.

not his worst qualities that got him into the worst trouble.

a sire, a bull for breeding, kept stabled, his eyes hooded, the movements of his legs hampered by thongs. He tramps restlessly, in darkness and confinement, no muscle permitted a sufficient range of movement in which to vent its powers. Held in abeyance, to be given freedom at the requisite moment, and burst forth in fury, a monster, bent upon rage, upon pleasure, upon assertion. To lie unused, to be fettered by lack of purpose, to champ, to rub weighty buttocks against the sides of the stall . . . to be called forth, bound upon some task . . .

a groveller, in boasting, must say that he would not be otherwise than he is.

do not watch him so uneasily, Woman. He will not approach your child. He is already disciplined in these matters.

stopped a stranger in the street and told him of my misfortunes, though he kept glancing in the direction of his appointment.

testamentum meum.

he might sally forth, try things as he chose—and if the situation became unbearable, he could announce that he was returning to his refuge. In this refuge all the old voices would be silenced—one could detect only such sounds as he had never heard before. The new sounds would be like gifts—he could hold them in his hands, or even lay his head against them.

had grammar, dialectic, and rhetoric as their trivium, yet knew so little about the deceptions of speech.

I went to her and turned her face to the light, but it was not Genevieve.

would not insist that we are, or are not, free to choose. But do insist that, when choosing, we cannot foresee all the factors involved in our choice—and how could a choice be called free when its conse-) *Aristotle~* quences are unknown at the time of our choosing?

The man did good for the oppressed? Then he made them oppressors.

A dream of Anthony. He referred on several occa- sions to his "exile," though it is I that was in exile. And without playfulness, he addressed me by his own name, nor did I find this unusual.

humbled that all negatives must be affirmed—for how advocate silence silently?

lapsing into the unformed.

if enough men could be brought to realize their plight, then we could at their instigation have a re-shuffling.

this pledge of fidelity: Were you, Genevieve, to return and by your sweetness to lift me from the entanglement into which I have got myself, were you to be the woman of a new era for me, in this new era I pledge fidelity. I should seek no further turmoil, not even were my life to lack freshness.

had he found the matter ludicrous, he could have spared himself much indignation.

now that she is gone, you cry out for her. But if she were with you, might you in some new way dismiss her?

could I, by a ritual, like the old Jews, load my sins upon a goat, I would beat it mercilessly and drive it into the wilderness to die.

each time I insulted them, they toasted me vociferously. They clamoured, huzzaed, pounded the table in delight. And finally, tiring of me, they pummelled me and pitched me from the room, though their good nature continued—and when I called for money they threw a few coins after me.

the practice, among conquering tyrants, of putting to death every twentieth man. Am I the victim of my attitudes, or a victim of vigesimation?

a few hours of abundance, to prepare for a lifetime of famine.

if decisions were a choice between alternatives, decisions would come easy. Decision is in the selection and formulation of alternatives.

I was but a harmless moth, made by its markings to look ferocious. I was a pumpkin to frighten children. Yet for this they have punished me.

have dreamed of Genevieve's return, but the nature of the dream confirms me in my fear that she is dead. Dreaming, I saw her in a mirror, where she spoke mirror words—and the flowers on her breast had mirror fragrance.

sitting on the same bench with me in the park . . .
they seemed like students . . . while listening to
their conversation I felt that I had things of importance to tell them . . . *"circulus vitiosus"* . . .
yet they resented my intrusion . . . otherwise I
should not have asked them for money.

if I could contrive some toy, such as a doll which,
by an inexpensive mechanism, could be made to act
insolently. Then I could take it to a man of enterprise—and if I were careful as to how the contract
was worded, I might get substantial returns from the
foolish thing.

they must train themselves in ingratitude, since
they can live only by taking alms from the enemy—and how is the enemy to be vanquished unless they are prepared to bite the hand that feeds
them?

there comes a time when one must abandon his vocabulary. For the rigidness of words, by discovering
a little, prevents us from discovering more. There is
a time for silence—not only outward silence, but
even the silencing of one's own thoughts. Soon I
shall open a door and pass through it, closing it

softly behind me—and thereupon I shall be sitting in a chamber of silence.

I vilified them, but they enjoyed me as a king enjoys his parrot or his dwarf. The more I attacked them, the noisier grew their delight.

If I became well known, and she were still alive, the newspapers would assist me by printing throughout the country the story of my search for her. But recall the Prince locked up in the Beast. She must find you before you are released to go in search of her.

became bat-blind, that he might have bat-vision.

resurgam! resurgam! I shall rise again! Hail, all hail! Here is a promise: *resurgam!*

stop and examine dark alleys, as Genevieve may be there.

though you, in learning, brought trouble upon yourself, let no man discredit your discoveries by pointing to your troubles. Nor must you turn against your bitterness. The sword of discovery goes before the couch of laughter. One sneers by the modifying of a snarl; one smiles by the modifying of a sneer. You should have lived twice, and smiled the second time.

could not escape misfortune unless they all did as I did.

what voices would one hear were the mind to be plunged into total silence? Were he to say nothing, not even in his thoughts—were he to live in the still-ness of a void—could he hear the cells of his body speaking? Might he distinguish the songs of the myriad little tenants in his blood, as we can con-template the pulsing sound of frogs rising above a marsh?

if they would let me stay about to amuse them, as the old kings kept dwarfs, I could say all kinds of scathing things to them that made them laugh—and each of them could tickle himself by prodding me to attack the others.

all I have pondered in malice, some one, coming after me, will consider comfortably. What I have learned through being in grave extremities, he will handle with ease.

Not only not responding, but even refraining from soliloquy—for if we tell no one, the grave burden accumulates within us. Henceforth silence, that the torrent may be heard descending in all its fulness.

THE END